THE HOTWELLS HORROR & OTHER STORIES

A FAR HORIZONS PUBLISHING ANTHOLOGY

IN MEMORY OF
DAVID J RODGER

ALL PROCEEDS FROM THE
SALES OF THIS BOOK GO TO
THE CHARITY MIND

MIND PROVIDE ADVICE AND SUPPORT
TO EMPOWER ANYONE EXPERIENCING
A MENTAL HEALTH PROBLEM. THEY
CAMPAIGN TO IMPROVE SERVICES,
RAISE AWARENESS AND PROMOTE
UNDERSTANDING.

The Hotwells Horror & other stories
Edited by Pete Sutton
First Edition Published
by Far Horizons Press
Jan 2018
This edition TBC

Contents

David J Rodger was born in Newcastle Upon Tyne in 1970 to an English father and Norwegian mother. He had 10 published novels set in a near-future world of corporate and political intrigue and was the creator of Yellow Dawn, a successful Role Playing Game based on the same world formed by his novels ten years after it has een devastated.

At the time of his death Yellow Dawn was in the final stages of being turned into a board game and also being scripted for a potential film. His partner of 14 years is looking to continue with this work with the help of his faithful RPG friends, so his legacy can live on.

He started writing at 19 and bought his first RPG at the tender age of 9 after begging his father for pocket money having spotted it with sheer delight in a shop window. This was the start of his love for H P Lovecraft and his first taste into the world of Cthulhu Mythos and the Dark Arts.

David moved to Bristol at 21 and the only delight on the long coach journey back to Newcastle was spending an hour in a Games Workshop at Birmingham New Street station. David joined many games & writing groups in Bristol and became quite prolific in the art scene. Over the years many a book launch or game event was held in coffee shops & cafes he frequented on more than a regular basis.

David's presence on the Internet got him a place in the BBC documentary Through the Eyes of the Young. He had also written non-fiction work for UK magazines and had short stories published in the UK, US, Canada & Japan. His final novel, Oakfield, was the first novel he started some 25 years earlier and was published just 7 months before his death. Acknowledgements were many which always included the masters of moods, musicians who created the essential atmosphere for his world.

He lived his final years with that Braun coffee maker, writing from a house on a hill with a view of the earth curve.

You can still find his work at www.davidjrodger.com

INTRODUCTION

I was aware of David before I met him. I'm not sure how,
some sort of writer's osmosis in the city I guess. But more
likely I'd seen his name on the BristolCon program. My first
appearance at BristolCon Fringe was with David. He read a Yellow
Dawn story. I'd researched him beforehand and knew that he'd do
something dark. Something dark pretty much describes my ouvre
and I thought that the audience may want some light relief so I
wrote an amusing story about amputation, which did get some
laughs. I remember David telling me that it was incredibly difficult
to get an audience to laugh – I've seldom tried it since. The same
evening David introduced Thomas David Parker to BristolCon
fringe – a fateful introduction I think since Tom now runs the
Fringe. Tom is one of the three without whom this book would not
exist. The other is Chris Halliday (more on him anon)

David and Tom had a firmer friendship than myself and David
but we continued to do events together – all three of us were
on the same program at Small Stories for example. And, as our
various stories explored similar dark spaces I suggested we do an
anthology, a triptych. The last email I have from David was on this
topic, looking forward to working together. But it was never to be.

But the idea of the anthology never went away. At the funeral
I spoke of it with Tom and Tom roped Chris in. Chris, again, was
a closer friend to David than I, or Tom even. Without Chris we
wouldn't have half the contributors we do.

From the start we wanted stories that David would have
enjoyed. I believe that's what we have. Within these covers
you'll find stories about topics David explored in his own work.
Lovecraftian tales and cyberpunk for sure but also a tale I hoped

would make him laugh, Hillraiser by Ken Shinn. Ken and David sadly never knew each other but I think they'd have got on well. Among the tales you'll find that Chris's Out of Context is a very fine story and very poignant, Tom's A Day at the Lake is one I think he'd discussed with David, Cheryl's Lovecraft tale would have tickled him I think. I've also included three of David's own tales which give a very brief insight into his writing – I recommend you go find more of it. Jo Garrard's introduction has a link where you can seek it out.

This book has been a long time in gestation, because it was a labour of love and paying work kept interrupting. For a long time the book was only ever referred to as 'For David' for that's what it is – a book in his memory, sure, but a book for him, wherever it is writers go when they pass from this world.

At the funeral we did a toast, in Norweigan and I'd like you, before going further with this book, to fetch yourself a glass of something strong and join us in another toast to David.

Og så svinger vi på seiddelen ingjen, hei skal!

(phonetically – Oh saw swinger vi paw saydelenn iyem, hey skawl!)

Peter Sutton (editor) September 2017

THE HOTWELLS HORROR

DAVID J RODGER

Investigation launched as 'unexplained' human remains discovered in Hotwells

B RISTOL: Police have launched an investigation after a member of the public found two bodies outside of one of the historic properties of the Colonnade.

Officers received the call at 8am on Sunday morning, from a person reporting human remains lying outside the front door, near to the main A4 Hotwell Road.

Subsequently, a further fourteen bodies have been discovered within six other properties at the Colonnade.

The deaths are currently being treated as unexplained, and an investigation has now been launched.

A huge police response was at Hotwells throughout the day on Sunday, with one lane of the A4 closed and the entire Colonnade cordoned off to the public, and officers conducting patrols.

Donald Collins, the force incident manager for Avon and Somerset Police, said: "At this moment in time we don't know how these people died. Itis too early in the investigation to make a useful statement, other than to say we do consider foul play to be involved.

"We were called at 8am this morning by a member of the public. I can confirm the bodies of a man and woman who were initially discovered.

"When officers began to canvass the neighbouring properties, further remains were discovered. A total of sixteen bodies have now been found.

"Crime Scene Managers have set up a mobile command centre in Hotwells and have begun their investigation."

Police have refused to confirm the nature of the victims' injuries, their age, or what they were wearing at the time they died, due to the potentially sensitive investigation.

It is the second 'unexplained incident' to take place in Hotwells over the weekend – three young men were taken to hospital on Saturday night after suffering some kind of gas-attack within their home on Christina Terrace which left them screaming and delirious. A fourth man was found dead inside the house, in a condition the policehave so far refused to comment on. All three men are in a critical condition.

Christina Terrace is only several hundred metresfrom the Colonnade.

The Colonnade curves into a cliff beside the Avon. Built as a shopping arcade for spa visitors in 1786, it is all that remains of the old Hotwell complex.

***

He found the box hidden in a secret compartment within the bathroom of the aged house; beneath the belly of the cast iron rolltop bath. It was a strange place to conceal it but Miloš suspected the large metal receptacle possibly helped to hide the box from those who had intended to find it first.

For him, the discovery was an accident, an intriguing surprise in the midst of a dull task, and the start of a brief mystery. A prelude to the horror.

He would soon come to wish to God he had never found it. Terrible consequences unfurled from that moment of blind curiosity.

The house belonged to his late uncle: Silas Smolák. He was there to clear the man's personal items and ensure the property was in a good condition for viewing and sale. There were no relatives to speak of. For either of them. Anyone who had been kin was now either dead or disowned from family fold.

Somewhat oddly, it had been eighteen months since his uncle passed away. Killed by a single, nerve-shredding stroke. Probate had taken forever to complete, delaying the proposed sale, due to complications over the estate. Specifically, when the firm of solicitors Quort, Menahem, Wexler had requested a detailed inventory of the dead man's things. This involved a thorough survey of the house in Sneyd Park, something which bizarrely included the use of expensive structure-penetrating radar, and thermal scannning equipment.

Had they been looking for the box? It was the first thought that came to Miloš's mind when he discovered it.

His discovery had occurred when he'd gone to clean the bathroom. He'd removed his wedding ring (wife long deceased) so it wouldn't snag on the flimsy rubber gloves he'd found beneath the kitchen sink. Placing the ring on the edge of the rolltop bath it had tumbled onto the floor, rolled and come to rest against the side of a low platform upon which the bath itself stood.

It was when he went to pick up the ring that he noticed it seemed to cling to the wood, not with any stickiness, but with a feeling of magnetic attraction. Which just didn't make any sense at all.

Miloš had knelt there, and played with the effect for a minute or so, holding the ring between his gloved fingers, moving it back and forth feeling the ring caught in some sort of field that exuded from the wooden platform... or from within it?

That was when he'd decided to find some tools to open up the platform and take a look.

Tucked away between two wooden joists was a rectangular box of smoky grey metal, reflective in a dull way, like pewter but not so soft.

Why had his uncle Silas hidden it there? What or who was he hiding it from? Quort, Menahem,Wexler? But who did they represent?

Reaching through the opening he had made, Miloš had lifted out the box, surprised by how heavy it was. He'd actually struggled to get it out.

But now he had it on the floor beside him.

Miloš sat there, with his back against the stud wall, the solid weight of the box resting across his thighs. The midmorning sun was streaming in through the small window above and to his left. The day was mild despite the lateness of year, and he felt comfortable, relaxed and warm.

The box was about the length of his forearm and almost as wide; quite deep, it had hinges concealed amongst elaborate decorative details. Miloš suspected the metal was not ordinary, and the unusual design suggested the box had a special purpose.

He was drawn to it, in a very particular way. It was as if it had some influence over him. A fact he was consciously aware of, but felt inclined to ignore. A palpable aura of risk: of hidden things, of secrets, locked away for good reason. Not to be opened. Not meant to be discovered at all.

Perhaps.

Or maybe it was intended to be found when the right person came along?

Was he the right person?

His mind felt off-balance; his thoughts jumbled and confused. He stared down at the box as if a great decision hung over him.

Strange...

There was no lock, just an ornate hasp mechanism. Making an abrupt decision he swung the lid open.

Inside he found the box contained a stack of paper documents and an object that initially looked like a fist-sized lump of quartz.

He examined the documents first.

Old sheets of paper that had been through a typewriter and some more modern laser-jet computer prints. No hydrogel or softscreen items, no so-called smart paper. Each document featured an ink-stamped reference to a certain Project Huld. Together they appeared to represent a historical record of construction carried out in the 19th century. Schematics and engineering diagrams showed cross-sections of a large shaft dug at a specific angle of elevation; complex machinery that looked like something from a Jules Verne story supposedly occupied this tunnel-like void.

Then Miloš realised what he was looking at and his roaming paused, his scalp tightened and a deep frown carved through his brow. The documents related to the Clifton Rock's Railway, but suggested the original structure had been created not as a railway but as the home of a magnificent, mysterious machine.

What the hell..?

He knew of Clifton Rocks Railway. It had opened in the 1890s, as far as he knew as a funicular to connect the lofty mansions of Clifton to Hotwells below. But these documents claimed the opening of the actual railway was planned with an intentional delay. A delay to allow the creation and activation of the machine called the qS-Probe.

Flicking through pages at random, Miloš learned the entire project was orchestrated by a group calling themselves the Large Cosmos Fraternity. It seemed this group had existed for centuries and Miloš's uncle had been a member of it, possibly a senior one. According to the paperwork Silas had been responsible for maintaining the ongoing operation of the machine and the measurements it continued to undertake, even after a century.

But what about the Clifton Rocks Railway? How could such a machine operate and remain hidden whilst the small funicular train line had been running? Miloš searched for answers in the documents.

Collusion between project members had kept those responsible for building the huge shaft and internal workings entirely in the dark. A fabricated complication over planning had facilitated the required delay. Nobody questioned it. Every person involved in the official construction felt they were merely doing their job, unaware they were facilitating the secret desires of the Large Cosmos Fraternity.

Once finished, the qS-Probe was activated and left to run.

Meanwhile, the public face of the Clifton Rocks Railway trundled into motion.

No details as to what the qS-Probe was measuring but there were clues.

Miloš was aware of a creeping discomfort sitting hunched over the box, its contents spreading across the bathroom floor.

***

He pulled everything together and moved downstairs. That was when he examined the curious quartz-like object. Standing by a small desk in his uncle's former study, Miloš held the item between both hands and slowly rotated it under the bright beam of a tall reading light.

It had a highly ordered property, as if perhaps it was made of crystal, and yet the weight of feel of it reminded him of a metal; also, there were angular protrusions, like thick, curving fronds, which were both artistic and yet seemingly functional - certainly they had been crafted, cut with a laser or some kind of energy that left perfect edges, creating an overall symmetry of form. It was pleasing to hold. As if he was wielding great power between his hands. He just didn't know what kind of power yet. Miloš went back to the documents.

Using his PA to run search queries through the Internet, he checked every name mentioned. He discovered that the original members of the Large Cosmos Fraternity consisted of a handful of exceptionally wealthy individuals with a background in Astronomy, Mathematics and Engineering, including electrical engineering - with references to the work of Bell, Bláthy, Edison, Ferraris, Heaviside, Hertz, Jedlik, Lord Kelvin, Parsons, Siemens, Swan, Tesla and Westinghouse. Other, less familiar and more esoteric names were listed, and searching through some of these revealed a shocking association to occult and paranormal studies of the late Victorian period.

It was unsettling, to think of so much money, effort and energy, wrapped in secrecy and dedicated to a machine that nobody had any awareness of. Nobody except the Fraternity.

Knowledge of the qS-Probe was handed down to successive members as generations passed.

None of the documents included details on current membership or their activity.

His uncle Silas seemed to be a missing link in a chain stretching back to the early-nineteenth century.

Why had he broken it?

The answer was there in black and white.

Final page in the stack of papers from the box; a handwritten letter, addressed to *"whoever finds this repository of lunacy & methodical stupidity"*.

It was rambling and chaotic, but the message in it was clear. A warning.

"Man's reckless push against the boundaries of places he should never venture will only lead to a catastrophic breach of the Quantisphere. From those places will come the hordes and minions of the Outer Chaos, creatures with wicked intellect and wild, relentless hunger. They will feast upon the warm blood and soft flesh like travellers gorging on milk and honey of a newly discovered land. And behind them, tumbling from the Void, such mercy I implore at what we have done. We have come close to oblivion. Listen to these words and pray to whatever god of yours may listen. Pray!"

Reading the entire letter placed a chill deep within Miloš's bones. It was fantastical and yet it appeared his uncle believed these events were entirely true.

The purpose of the machine built by the Large Cosmos Fraternity was to fire an energy beam that could probe the outermost layers of the fabric of the universe. Not the edge of the universe itself but the shape of the dimensions that bound it together. The machine existed out of phase with mundane reality. Its physical structure had been shifted onto a higher-plane, allowing it to coexist for a century and more with the Clifton Rocks Railway. The railway had never run at a profit and closed a few decades after opening - a situation ascribed to the unusual energy (and mood) radiated by the machine's operation.

The motive behind building machine was apparently an academic one. To 'map' higher-dimensional space.

According to the letter in Miloš's hand, the project was, and continued to be, a success; providing the Fraternity with a drip-feed of sometimes explosive data. Tantalising hints about the structure and forms beyond the known dimensions. His uncle's role required him to regularly visit the machine's control room, ensure calibrations were in order and retrieve the latest measurements. The fist-sized object from the box was in fact the key that allowed a custodian to step up, out of mundane reality, into the control room which, like the machine itself, existed in a sort of no-place on the edges of our universe.

The machine was still here. Just out of phase with the physical world around it.

This is where the letter took on a strange and disturbing tone.

About three months before his death, his uncle became aware of new phenomenon when he climbed up into that "control room" within the no-place. Initially he put it down to imagination, or some periodic output of the machine, but over successive visits he became aware of an increasing feeling of being observed; as if something was watching him from a great distance, a distance that was shrinking. Then came sounds - a deep, chord-like thrumming, as if an enormous piano string had been struck and the sound was reverberating through limitless gulfs of space to strike the walls. The control room was never detailed in the letter, although Miloš did find references to it in some of the engineering drawings; triangular in shape, with a wedge-like profile in height... wrought iron panels held together with industrial rivets. His uncle described his last visit to the no-place.

"The corners of that black chamber were no longer visible but merely intersecting curves... the longer I stared the less anything I was seeing made any sense. This room is a terrible construct, a mote in the eye of a great beast that must surely blink and dig some awful appendage to pluck and claw this thing away. I cannot return here any longer. I do not believe it is safe. The sounds that vibrate the walls, a pulsing beat of an approaching horror. It is coming. Our beam has touched something... out there, beyond...it has taken an interest and now it is following this damned machine back to the source. It is coming and if we open a way from our world to this no-place then not even Hell will have refuge for our damned souls."

The letter stated how his uncle had tried to warn the Fraternity but nobody wanted to listen. When he locked down the no-place and hid the key, they threatened him.

Miloš stared at the lengthy letter between his fingers, aware that his hands were trembling. His gaze drifted to the object he'd placed on the small table near the lamp.

There was an implication in the dead man's words. That his life had come into danger; that grim-faced forces were lining up against him.

All of this seemed so far-fetched that Miloš considered whether it wasn't some sort of elaborate hoax; or if his uncle had simply gone mad.

Yet he had the object, the so-called key. If there was one way to find out for certain if there was even the slightest shred of truth to this nonsense, it was to take the key and go to the place it supposedly opened.

***

It was late afternoon. The sky was cloudless and pastel blue, the sun skimming low along the autumnal horizon to cast long shadows. Sneyd Park was an oasis of quiet streets, hedgerows, managed trees and small mansions. The air was already growing chilly and smelled of damp leaves. Miloš carried the box and its contents to his car; dumped them in the boot, everything except the key which he kept with him.

He drove across the Downs, then down Blackboy Hill, Whiteladies Road and Queens Road, filtering right to get onto Jacob's Wells where thousands had been buried in open pits after the Black Death decimated Medieval England. He had always found this area suffered from an odd aura, a slightly oppressive atmosphere that lingered even on warm sunny days. Now he wondered if it was something to do with this machine which wasn't that far distant.

Jacob's Wells took him down onto Hotwells Road, a main thoroughfare that was itself a bottle-neck as it squeezed between the natural basin of the landscape and the urban developments stacked alongside.

It took nearly an hour to find a parking place and it was almost dark. Miloš left the car on Christina Terrace, beneath the imposing terrace of properties that rose up like a claustrophobic wall of brick, old windows and sagging roofs of grey slate. Carrying only the quartz-like lump of the key, he strolled towards the nearby harbour, and followed the edge onto the Portway; street-lights reflecting off the deep water.

The Portway, a thin strip of blacktop crowded with vehicles, was a chaotic continuation of the main thoroughfare, pressed tightly between the edge of the river and the mighty rock cliffs that formed Clifton Gorge. River and gorge meandered several miles towards the cargo port of Avonmouth.

The entrance to Clifton Rocks Railway was only a short walk along this Portway, just past a curving row of Georgian buildings known as the Colonnade. Quaint in architecture and aspect, they suffered terribly from the tens of thousands of vehicles that trundled past each day. A black grime clung to every surface and Miloš could feel his lungs soaking up the stinking fumes.

It was strange to be a pedestrian here, forced to walk a narrow pavement only metres from such heavy traffic,

Headlights pushing away the gloom but creating a churning flow of shadows.

Moving beyond the Colonnade the pavement became nothing more than a cycle lane, cars and trucks whooshing past within reaching distance to his left, and the near vertical wall of the gorge, brushing against his right shoulder, rising up vertically nearly 100 metres. There was an immense sense of being dwarfed by scale, and insignificant against the volume of vehicles.

And yet...

Miloš felt the weight of the key clenched within his fist, its metallic crystal aspect and irregular yet crafted protrusions digging into the flesh of his palm and fingers. A power existed here. He had no doubt now. There was an acute sense of the physical world around him responding to the key's presence, shifting.

The doorway to Clifton Rocks Railway was ahead of him. Rusting metal bars in a rusting metal frame; apparently locked, Miloš wasn't concerned.

At first it had just been the absence of shadows, a change in the way the headlights and taillights of the traffic affected the wall of gorge around the doorway. Then he saw there was another doorway superimposed upon this one. An outline sketched in vague illumination that Miloš couldn't tell was from a light source or the incandescence of heat.

The air around him appeared to buckle and shimmer, as if boiling, but did not affect his breathing or burn his skin. He continued to walk forward, passing through the corroded metal bars as if they did not exist. Or as if perhaps he no longer existed on the same physical plane. He was apparently within the walls of the gorge. Darkness framed by edges of heat and light. A tunnel that ascended in a giant sweeping curve, yet walking forwards felt like descending an angled ramp. There was a smell like burned sugar and engine oil. Sounds crackled in his ears, often distant but sometimes very close within the looming darkness. Against this was a background of mechanical humming, as if a cyclopean generator was at work some astronomical distance away.

He continued to walk, his pace becoming a full stride as fear diminished and confidence grew. Optical distortions created tiny flares of light and vision of the tunnel twisting in a spiralling shape that broke all laws of rationality and logic.

Up ahead, if that term even made sense now, was the notion of a room forming. Outlines oozing through the darkness to knit together into a solid structure. It was as if he was looking down at the schematics of a constructed place from above, seeing it as well as seeing through it. He was striding forward yet descending, coming closer.

But Miloš began to perceive the room wasn't forming correctly. The corners where the edges of black metal walls intersected kept writhing and squirming, bulging and bubbling as if being manipulated into some other shape.

Miloš began to slow his stride as the thought reached him:

It was as if something on the other side was forcing itself up against the metal...trying to break through.

Miloš stopped, suddenly wanting to turn away and run. To flee. Yet a gruesome fascination had a hold of him. He wanted to know more. He wanted to see what this place was and what his uncle had become so fearful of.

It came from within an abrupt protrusion ahead of him, like boil of glistening greyness pushing out from the black nothingness of this no-place. A sinewy, hairless thing with a long anaemic tail and a vague resemblance to a hound, tumbled from that sphere like a slime-covered suckling spilling from the burst womb of a dead mother. The stench washed over him and nearly knocked him flat. Scrambling up onto writhing, insect-like limbs, the monstrous hound snapped the gelatinous mass of its head towards him, as if smelling or sensing him. Contrails of evaporating slime followed in the wake of its movements, like smoke rising from a fire. The thing was semi-solid, made of a dark matter, outlines pulsing with a repulsive ultraviolet colour.

Featureless, the head was just a horrible blunt ovoid of ridges, now flickering with more of the ultraviolet. The head angled to one side, fixed on him, as the rest of the body cautiously circled around; it was lining up to attack.

Miloš staggered backwards, half-falling, and managed to turn and stumble into a run. Gagging and choking out a scream of terror, his arms pumped by his sides as he forced his legs to carry him faster from this nightmare.

It chased him on multiple limbs, large claws held up, whilst spongy, slime-coated paws made almost no sound.

Running full-tilt. Vague glimpse of headlights up ahead. Growing stronger as he neared the exit point. He still had the key clenched within his hand. It was now his only weapon if the thing behind him tried to strike.

Something punched through him. From behind. Like a spear. That then ripped backwards, tearing parts of him with it. The strength vanished from Miloš's legs and he tumbled to the non-existent floor.

Lying there on his back, propped up on elbows, he gasped for breath with a horrible wheezing, gurgling sound. Clutching the key, he watched helpless as the hound padded towards him; stooped, head lowered and jutting forward...whilst a ghostly tongue or proboscis snaked in and outwards of the featureless face.

That tongue dripped with a sticky red fluid, and Miloš realised with dismay that it was his blood. The hound was tasting it, savouring it.

Miloš glanced behind him, crying out in pain, and saw that the exit point was only a few metres away. He could crawl, he was sure... but what then?

The hound came up to him and then slithered over him where he lay, forcing Miloš to flop down onto his back. The freakish, semi-solid surface of its hide smeared off onto his clothes like a luminous paste, glaring ultraviolet and pulsing black. Miloš cried out, instinctively raised his hands, one wrapped around the key, and tried to push the hound off him.

As soon as his flesh came into contact with the vile body, his skin went ice cold and appeared to melt away, blistering, darkening, separating and then becoming a bluish smoke that drifted from the exposed bones. Miloš made a shrill, high--pitch howl of agony and terror, wanting to disbelieve what his eyes were showing him. But he was literally turning into vapour where he was sprawled. Tiny breathing holes, inverted pustules, quivered open in the flanks of the hound and inhaled the puffs of blue smoke coming from his demise. It was consuming him. Feeding from him.

The key dropped away from what was left of his hand.

But he no longer cared.

His legs thrashed. His body tried to turn. But the grotesque stains the thing had left across him were now eating through his clothes.

He died in the vague wash of headlights sweeping along the Portway, as the hound scooped up the key within a monstrous fore-claw and then swung its sensory organs towards the open doorway.

INTERNAL MEMO – HAND DELIVERY ONLY

Large Cosmos Fraternity

From: Sampson Nikolajsen

To: all LCF members

Re: Purple Dawn Foundation

I am preparing a summary of conclusions and actions following an investigation into the Hotwells incident. Investigation was completed by Albin Holst, with assistance from the Purple Dawn Foundation - as per discussion between Grand Master and Senior Secretary on the matter of integrity versus security. The Foundation has been forthright in their opinions and has not held back on help, where it has been required. However, they do hold the LCF entirely at fault for the incident in Hotwells and insist that funds are set aside to assist the families that have been affected, and to any that may be affected in the future as the incident is not entirely closed.

You may not be aware that Wassim Umbra, director the Foundation, travelled from Egypt with a member of his staff on loan from the Miskatonic University in America. They visited the site of the qS-Probe and were able to re-render the gateway, in so far as it was necessary without actually opening it. The Foundation has sealed the gateway with enchantments and wards. This way is now closed, and the machine is lost to us. Umbra was hoping to attend a meeting of the Quorum but he has to return to Giza due to a crisis of global magnitude.

Hotwells was lucky. Something much greater in magnitude was breaking through the fabric of the control room. Umbra explained that ahead of it came something related to the Hounds of Tindalos that occupy the angles of time and roam the spaces between the curves of different planes. Whatever came through the gateway did the damage it did before seeking shelter at dawn. It has slipped away into some place within Hotwells but not a part of Hotwells.

It is still there, however, and so may reappear at some point. Umbra intends to send one of his team to meet with me and Holst to review a plan to tackle this. It will not be easy. We have caused a fracture in the membrane that binds our world together and protects it. In essence, the LCF must come to an end. We have learned much, about the fragile nature of reality but we pushed too hard, too far into territories we should actually fear to tread!

I will send through the full report in due course.

Xiku Xikoth – *Provenance!*

Sampson Nikolajsen

OUT OF CONTEXT
CHRIS HALLIDAY

When the phone rings after midnight, it's almost never a good sign. Since when has a late night phone call ever been the start of something nice? I was still struggling to get my brain into gear when I heard Martin on the other end of the line. "Kyle? I think I've been hacked," he muttered, not bothering to be social. Martin Harper was what we euphemistically refer to as 'on the spectrum', - high-functioning but socially oblivious.

"Martin," I grumbled. "Fuck, mate, it's like..." I glanced at the bedside clock. "It's two-fucking-thirty. AM!"

"I've been hacked," he said again, completely ignoring the irritation in my voice that I was doing nothing to hide.

"I don't care if you've been mugged by the Virgin Mary. It's the middle of the bloody night."

Now, you're going to ask me if I always swear this much. Of course I fucking do. What sort of question is that? Pay attention.

I could hear Martin's breathing over the phone, and it occurred to me that it was wrong, somehow, fast and shallow, like he'd been running. *Or,* the thought percolated through my annoyance, *like he's scared.*

"Martin, are you okay?"

"Someone's been at my photos."

"How'd you mean?"

"There's something wrong with my photos. Someone's messed about with them."

"Which photos, mate?"

"All of them."

I guess I should explain, otherwise this is going to make even less sense to you than it did to me at the time. Martin liked photos. He took a lot of them. His parents had died about five years ago, and since then he'd become almost obsessed with photographically documenting every aspect of his life. You couldn't have a latte with him without him snapping a shot of you with foam all over your top lip. When he'd started off, he'd been an indifferent photographer, but he was getting better, and there were some really lovely shots in his online gallery. If some nasty little script-kiddie had messed with them, it was no wonder he was upset.

I dug deep, mustered the few brain cells I could find, and sat up, switching the bedside light on. Next to me, Kerrie grumbled incoherently and tunnelled deeper into the duvet. I didn't have to worry about waking her up; she could sleep for England and get the gold.

"Has someone hacked your photo stream?"

"I think so, yeah."

"How do you know?"

"Because there's something wrong with my pictures. All of them. It's like a watermark or something."

"Hang on, mate." I took the phone from my ear, plugged in the ear buds and then scrolled off the main screen until I found the short cut to Martin's gallery. My Wi-Fi is slower than the economy, so it took a few seconds for the page to load. "Alright, I'm looking at your gallery. Which pictures was it?"

"All of them!" He sounded pissy, as if he couldn't stand how long it was taking me to get it. I considered telling him to get fucked and going back to sleep, but my curiosity was roused now. I tapped a photo icon and it filled my phone screen.

"Okay, I'm looking at that shot of us at your birthday last year. What am I looking for?"

"In the background."

"Where in the background?"

"Just fucking look!" That brought me up short. Martin was intense, yes, and frequently annoying, but he was also very proper. Martin never swore. Like, *ever*. I'd seen him accidentally put his hand through a pane of glass and all he said was "Oops!" So I looked.

I remembered the picture well. I'd picked it because it was a good one of Kerrie and I. We'd been happily sloshed and we were gazing at each other with the sort of adoring puppy-face that everyone but a loved-up couple gets heartily sick of very quickly. Martin had caught us entirely unaware, wrapped up in each other, and it showed.

It took a few seconds before I realised what was wrong. There was an odd distortion in the picture, just over my left shoulder. A weird symmetric pattern, like a butterfly, just hanging in the air. The more I looked at it the easier it was to see. Martin was right. It *did* look like a watermark.

"You see it, don't you?"

"I think so, mate, yeah. Like a butterfly?"

"Or a fractal, yes."

"And it's in every photo?"

"All the ones with me in, yes."

Hang on, I thought. "But you're not in this one."

"Look in the window," he said. He suddenly sounded very tired. I looked, and there he was, reflected in the glass of the window behind us. I'd looked at this picture uncounted times and never noticed him there before.

Beside me Kerrie grumbled again. I turned off the bedside lamp and slid out of bed, using the glow of my phone to navigate out of the room. I snagged a dressing gown on the way out and closed the bedroom door quietly behind me before padding into my study.

"So," I said, picking my words carefully. "You reckon that someone has hacked your gallery and watermarked every photo with you in? Not every photo, just the ones with you in?"

"Yeah." Again, he sounded tired, as if the initial flush of adrenaline and anger was wearing off.

"Well, it sucks, but you know what to do. Change your passwords and restore from back-up."

"I can't." His voice cracked a little, here, for all the world as if he was about to cry.

"Why not?"

"Because it's on the back-ups too."

I sat for a moment, trying to process what he was saying. Martin was the king of digital media. He loved to travel, and hated having physical stuff tying him down if he could help it. But after losing one of the last emails his mum had sent him in a hard-drive crash a few years ago, he was paranoid about his back-ups. He had multiple copies of everything; in the cloud, on portable hard-drives, on social media sites, everywhere. There was no way some hacker could have compromised all of them. It didn't make sense.

I sat at my desk and nudged my laptop into life. The screen glowed and emitted a soft chime as the hard-drive spun up, and I tapped in my password. Martin fretted in my ears as I moused around my desktop until I found my pictures folder. I clicked it open and scrolled through the icons until I found what I was looking for. The picture filled my screen, and I felt a cold chill trickle down my spine.

"Fuck me," I muttered.

"What is it?"

"It's on my copy too." But it couldn't be. It simply couldn't be. The copy I had was a hi-res version Martin had sent me after his birthday, and the watermark or whatever it was hadn't been there before. But it was there now.

Martin was quiet for a moment. Then he seemed to stutter back into life. "How's that possible? A worm, maybe?"

I shrugged, before realising that he couldn't see me. "Fucked if I know. I'll tell you something though; this isn't just some script-kiddie. If he's hacked your stream and your back-up and my box, he's a clever bugger. And why would he do it anyway? You take nice pictures, but it's not like you're Ansell Adams."

"Who?"

"Philistine. I mean you're not anyone special, you know?"

"Thank you, Captain Charm School," Martin chided.

"Go fuck yourself. You know what I mean."

"Fair point." Martin paused for a moment, then said "why is it only the pics with me in?"

"Maybe he just doesn't like you. Maybe he's trying to make a point. He could just be showing off. Have you checked your email?"

"Yeah," Martin muttered. "No demands for money with menaces if that's what you mean."

"So it's not ransomware."

"Don't think so."

There was a moment of silence between us. A crackle of static fuzzed the line for a moment while I looked at the screen of my laptop. I leaned closer. "It's funny," I said after a beat. "It's easier to see in high-res."

"I know."

"But that doesn't make sense."

"Why not?" Martin sounded disinterested, as if he was now lost in the thought of how he could recover or repair his image archive.

"Because surely if this is a watermark, the resolution of the picture it's on isn't going to affect it. The watermark is going to look the same on all the pictures. But this...whatever it is looks sharper on the high-res version of this picture than it does on the web-resolution one you've got up on your gallery."

"And?"

"And that's either a very clever watermark, or..." My voice trailed off as my thoughts raced ahead, but Martin got there first.

"...or it's not a watermark at all," Martin finished for me.

"Have you got any hard copies?" I asked, suddenly feeling very, very odd indeed, like the world was turning a corner that I couldn't clearly see and didn't understand.

"You know I don't do physical media."

"And now you've been compromised, genius," I shot back. "Luckily, some of us are a little smarter." I pulled open a desk drawer and rummaged around in it until I found a stack of photos and pulled them out. Quickly I flicked through them. And then I stopped.

I always used to laugh at the clichéd descriptions of fear in stories. Fear, I used to believe, couldn't really feel like icy fingers down the spine, or being drenched in cold water. But then, I'd never really felt fear until tonight. One of the things the descriptions miss out is the metallic taste that fills your mouth. It's not the warm coppery taste of blood, or the hard tang of steel. It's sharp and cold and slightly acidic, as if your saliva has curdled under your tongue.

I sat for a moment, my mouth full of that unfamiliar taste, the tips of my fingers tingling as if the blood in my hands had decided to go somewhere safer. I was looking at a slightly dog-eared photo that Kerrie had taken of Martin and me two years ago. We were sitting in a pub, faces flushed and wind-burned after attempting our first and last half-marathon. I had my foot up on a stool, proudly displaying a blister the size of a duck's egg, and Martin was doing the 'rabbit ears' behind my head, just like he did in every photograph of us together. In the cheap flock wallpaper behind us, was a faint shape, like a butterfly.

"Kyle, man, you're freaking me out." Martin's voice was trembling.

"I, er..." My throat was dry, and I couldn't get the words out. I swallowed hard and tried again. "It's on the hard copies."

"You're kidding me."

"Martin, I'm not kidding."

"This isn't funny!"

"Jesus, Martin, I swear to God, I'm not fucking about. I'm looking at the print of the pic Kerrie took of us after the fun run, and it's there. It's right. Fucking. *There*."

"That's not possible." Martin's breathing had picked up again, and by that point so had mine.

"I know it's not possible. I also know that I'm looking right at it."

There was a pause, then Martin said "What about the others?" I quickly flicked through the other pictures in the stack, and there it was. In every picture I had of Martin, there was the butterfly shape. In some photos it looked like a watermark, while in others it seemed to be a shadow. Occasionally it just looked like an optical illusion, the collision of light and shade conspiring to form a shape from random elements.

I spread the photos out on the desk in front of me and studied them. "It's in all of them. Every photo I have of you, it's there." I tracked back through the pictures, checking each one again. By the time I'd looked at them all again, I knew there was something else. "Martin?"

"Yeah?"

"It's getting bigger."

"No."

"I'm not kidding, mate. If I put these pics in chronological order, it looks like it's either getting bigger, or..."

"Don't say it."

"... or it's getting closer."

There was a long, long pause after that. Martin's breathing kicked up a notch, and I could imagine him alone in a darkened room, staring at his phone. I wanted to say something, but the words kept colliding in my head, like a panicked crowd trying to leave a building by a single exit and getting tangled up.

"So... what is it?" Martin's voice made me jump, and broke the reverie I'd been sliding into.

"I don't know," I said. "Let's break it down. It's on every photo of you that I can find, digital and physical. It's either getting bigger or closer to the camera in every shot as it gets closer to today. It looks like a butterfly..."

"Or a fractal," Martin interrupted.

"... Or a fractal," I conceded.

"And it's impossible."

"And," I agreed, "It's impossible."

"Well, that was productive." Martin tried to laugh, but the sound broke a little in his throat. He was close to losing it, I think, and so was I.

"Okay, so it's impossible. Maybe we're looking at it wrong?"

"Explain," he said.

"Well, if what it looks like is impossible, maybe we're not understanding it right? I mean, it looks like a frigging watermark or something, on every picture of you, even pictures that it wasn't previously on. That's clearly impossible, so maybe there's another explanation."

"A hoax? Someone's dicking us about?" He sounded hopeful at that, and I hated to let him down.

"Mate, for someone to be hoaxing us, they'd have to be a genius hacker and have somehow altered or replaced all my physical photos. Unless you've pissed off a bloody supervillain, I think we both know that's not an option. No, I mean what if what it looks like isn't what it actually is." I was speaking slowly, drawing the words out to give the ideas that were rolling around in my mind time to crystallise. It wasn't that what I was thinking was particularly difficult to grasp. It's just that it was crazy. It's funny though. Looking back on that night, I'm not even sure anymore that they were my ideas. I remember the feeling of them, plunking into my consciousness like stones in a pond. Now I find myself wondering where they came from.

"What... what if it's not actually in the photos?"

"Kyle, I can see it."

"Yeah, and so can I. Bear with me though. Maybe it's not actually there on the paper or in the file. Maybe it's kind of... *between*... them and us?"

"I have no clue what you're trying to say."

"I know, mate. I'm trying to get my head around this as well." I took a deep breath, and then plunged on. "What if it's something contextual? Like, it doesn't exist in the real world, but in the information *about* the real world. Like metadata."

Martin laughed. It was high-pitched and strained, and it didn't sound like him at all. We laughed a lot, he and I, but this sound wasn't anything I wanted to hear from him.

"You've lost it, mate."

"You've read Dawkins, right? The Selfish Gene?"

"So?"

"You remember the chapter on memes? When he talks about the biological behaviour exhibited by ideas? That they multiply and spread and mutate, just like bacteria?"

"Yeah, I remember. So you're saying that my photo archive has been vandalised by an idea?" He sounded incredulous now, and more than a little annoyed. I wondered briefly if he thought I wasn't taking this seriously. I was, and what's more, I was bloody terrified.

"Where does an idea live, Martin? Where does information exist?"

"It... Information's not a *thing*. It's like..." His voice trailed off. I could almost hear his brain ticking over, grappling with the concept. I pushed further.

"Does it exist purely on paper? Or does it exist in our heads alone? If you kill everyone who knows about an idea, and burn every record of it, do you destroy it, or do you just make it temporarily inaccessible?"

"You're seriously freaking me out, Kyle."

"I read a theory once that suggested that everything is ultimately information. I mean, we're genetic information, decoded and expressed by our cells, right?" My mind was racing now, the words tumbling out of my mouth. "Dawkins didn't go far enough. Jesus. He was speculating about ideas being like bacteria, but bacteria evolve. Everything started from bacteria. We started from bacteria. Bacteria implies an eco-system and an eco-system implies... oh, fuck."

"What?" Martin's voice was urgent. "What does it imply?"

My mouth was dry. Suddenly the room felt a lot colder and darker than it had before. "An eco-system implies predators."

"Are you saying this thing is stalking me?"

"Maybe," I said. "But if I'm right, it's not really in the pictures. It's in the meaning of the pictures. It's in our perception of them, of what they contain."

"What they all contain is me." Martin went quiet, for a moment, the contact between us marred briefly by a sudden crackle of static that made me jump. "What does it want?"

I pondered that for a while. "Well, if it's an idea, maybe it eats information? Maybe it's feeding off some of the information you generate, just by existing. Like a shark following a fishing boat and feeding on the cast-offs. Maybe to it we're like storms, stirring up the depths of the information sea, bringing up all the little fishes and plankton."

There was another burst of static, and Martin said something I couldn't hear. I got him to repeat it, and my heart went cold.

"But you said we're information." He sounded very calm now, very considered. "We're just genetic information, right? Instructions encoded in chemicals and unpacked by our cells at the right time. We're just walking blueprints. What happens if that information goes away?" The line crackled again, as if somewhere a storm was interfering with the signal.

"Kyle?"

"Yeah mate?"

"There's something on the wall."

"What do you mean?"

"In my bedroom. There's a shape on my wall. Like a shadow, but I can't see what's casting it." His voice cracked, and the next words were almost obscured by static, but I think they were "it's like a butterfly."

The line went dead.

I swore and hit the recent calls button to call him back, then stopped short. His name wasn't there. According to my phone, my last incoming call had been Kerrie, when she'd called to ask me what I fancied for dinner. *Glitch*, I thought, and started scrolling through my contacts. Martin's name wasn't there either.

I want you to try and imagine how I felt then, sitting in a darkened room with my laptop humming in front of me, dressed in nothing but a threadbare dressing gown I'd stolen from a hotel in Naples, looking for my friend's number on a phone I'd used to call him hundreds of times, and not finding it.

I started to feel sick, as if I was on a ship in the high seas, and the deck was rolling beneath my feet. I put the phone down on the desk, on top of the photos, and stared at it, waiting for Martin to call me back. He didn't call, and after a moment my eyes wandered to the photos. That's when I felt my heart skip a beat. Yes, I know it's a cliché, but that's what it felt like. Even clichés have to be true sometime, right?

The... thing – the watermark or fractal or whatever it was – had gone. And so had Martin.

I grabbed the pile of photos and started flicking through them, slowly at first, then faster and faster, over and over again. Me after the fun run. Me at the pub. Me at a party. Me with Kerrie... and no-one else. Photos I knew had been of Martin and me, now held only me.

I only just made it to the bathroom before the bile that had been roiling around my stomach came gushing up out of my mouth. I was shaking and I kept heaving into the toilet, over and over, until I felt empty and cold and wrung out. When I was done I brushed my teeth and rinsed out my mouth, acting almost instinctively. My face in the mirror was pale, and I couldn't hold my own gaze.

I was almost dressed when Kerrie peered out from under the duvet. "Wass goin' on?"

"I've got to go out." I couldn't look at her. She'd have seen the fear in my eyes.

"Iss early," she mumbled, looking at the clock. She didn't really do mornings. "Come back t'bed."

"I'll be back soon," I said. "I'm just going to see Martin."

"Who?"

I practically ran from the flat.

Martin's place was only a short drive away. He lived in a little Victorian terrace near the university, bought with the money his parents had left him. He wasn't terribly social and tended to talk to women as if they were mildly curious specimens from another planet, so he lived alone. I'm pretty sure I was flashed by a speed cam on the way over, but at that point I really didn't care.

I pulled up outside Martin's place, parked badly and ran up the stairs to his front door. I rang the bell, but no-one answered. Then I started banging on the door. Eventually next door's hall light came on and their front door opened. A very pissed off looking woman stared at me. "Do you know what time it is?"

"Er, I'm sorry," I pleaded, trying to sound harmless. "I'm worried about my friend. I had a phone call, and now he won't answer the door."

"Of course he won't answer the door. There's nobody there!"

"Has he gone out?"

She looked at me like I'd sprouted an extra eye in the middle of my forehead. "Nobody lives there. It's been empty for months. Previous tenants left at the end of term."

I glanced up at the brass numbers on Martin's front door. It was the right address. "Are you sure?"

She sighed theatrically. "No, I'm just making it up because I like having conversations on my doorstep in the middle of the bloody night!"

I held my hands up and backed away, my stomach sinking. "I... I'm really sorry. I must have got the wrong street." Then I turned and bolted for my car, feeling the woman's eyes on my back as I ran.

It's gotten worse since then. No one seems to remember Martin. Mutual friends, relatives... no one. His digital footprint has vanished. I can't find records of him anywhere. I went back to his place in the daylight and there was no sign of him. All his stuff was gone, and the house looked like it had been unoccupied for months. Kerrie and I had our first big argument because she didn't understand that he was gone. He *introduced* us, and now she doesn't know who he is. She thinks I'm messing her about, like it's all some stupid practical joke that I don't know when to drop. No one remembers him at all.

Except me.

I've been walking around in a daze since that night. Kerrie keeps looking at me oddly, as if she thinks I might be going mad. Maybe I am? She tries to understand and be supportive, God bless her, but what if I really am going crazy? What if Martin never actually existed?

I'm so scared now, all the time. I keep thinking about what took Martin, about what may have happened to him. I keep thinking about that shadow, unfurling like a Venus flytrap or a deep sea octopus, drawing him in and... eating his information, unravelling him somehow. I keep thinking about the fact that you can't really destroy information. I keep dreaming about him, about the possibility that something monstrous ate him and that in some horrible way he's still alive inside it.

And I keep thinking about why it is that I remember him, and it.

Maybe it does spread like a disease. Maybe it needs an infection vector. Maybe it needs to breach our defences before it can hunt us. Maybe that's why I can remember.

You see, there's a mark on my wall. A shadow, and I can't see what casts it.

It looks like a butterfly.

A DAY AT THE LAKE

THOMAS DAVID PARKER

Metta closed her eyes and started her playlist. Soon the comforting sound of Green Day filled her ears as the world began to melt away. She had gone for a hike to a lake with her husband, but things hadn't gone to plan.

It had taken them hours to get there. Her husband enjoyed hiking and had found a scenic trail he wanted to try out. Unfortunately, he neglected to mention it was up the side of a mountain. Literally, the side of a mountain. He told her that it would be worth it, but as the day wore on, Metta and her blistered feet became less and less convinced. The plan had been to find a nice remote place to enjoy the beautiful sunshine. However, when they reached the lake they discovered it was already busy, a crowded tourist spot. There was even a shop selling souvenirs.

Metta was not pleased. She looked at her husband as he desperately tried to put a positive spin on the situation, but he knew it was hopeless.

"Is this your idea of a quiet romantic getaway?" She said, goading him.

"Well, it looked pretty isolated on the map, I didn't think that many people would find it," he replied sheepishly.

"There's a fucking road, Christopher!" Metta gestured to the smooth asphalt that led to the neatly maintained car park. Christopher admitted defeat and apologised.

However, just as he began to explain that he hadn't realised the road came all this way it looked too narrow for cars on the map, he was silenced by the roar of a bus engine. Metta stared at him in furious silence as a herd of tourists disembarked and their screaming kids headed for the water.

The tension was palpable, and the only thing that saved him was his obvious mortification. As angry as she was, Metta couldn't help but pity her poor husband as she saw his romantic plans fall apart.

She hated that. How his poor puppy dog expression always made her sympathetic, when what she really wanted him to do was crawl away and die. Well, maybe not die, but find a way to fix things. She felt frustrated and his hang-dog expression just made things worse. It was hard staying mad at him when he was so apologetic, and that made her even more furious.

Fortunately, he knew one quick way to appease her and so he went to the shop to buy her cigarettes. Meanwhile, quietly fuming, Metta sat alone at a picnic table and began watching the various groups of people at the water's edge.

There were the screaming kids, probably pissing and shitting in the water, and running around in such a wild fashion that sooner or later they would harm themselves. Their oblivious parents would probably try to blame someone else for the injury. New parents have such an amazing ability to ignore the shortfalls in their own child rearing skills. The dicks.

Then there were the group of doddering old people, probably also pissing and shitting in the water, but now shuffling around in such an irritating fashion that they too would fall over and injure themselves. Of course, everyone would run to help because, that's what was expected. Metta furtively hoped they would collide with the children, wiping each other out. The dicks.

And finally, there were the young beautiful couples a bit further down, their bodies so pristine that they probably never had to piss or shit in their entire lives. Laughing and joking and running around in a conspicuous fashion that demonstrated they were too graceful to fall over. Their lives were perfect and they were oblivious to anything that wasn't. The dicks.

That was why Metta resorted to closing her eyes and listening to Green Day. Everything was better when she listened to Green Day. They were the best band in the world and, sure enough, her mood began to improve. Idly, she imagined a monster from the bottom of the lake rising up and devouring the crowd. It was glorious.

Soon, Christopher returned with the cigarettes. He had bought an ice cream and an inflatable lilo too. His heart was in the right place, Metta thought, although a bit simple at times and all too eager to please. They walked for a while and settled down on a small section of the shore that was removed from the crowds. It was slightly muddy, but firm enough that they could sit and not sink. They sat on their bags to keep their clothes clean and ate their ice creams in awkward silence. Metta's residual anger was ebbing away, but she still hadn't quite forgiven Christopher. He seemed to know this instinctively, so rather than say anything, he resorted to blowing up the lilo.

Metta watched him huff and puff while she gently sucked on her cigarette. His shoulders were rising and falling with each deep breath. She watched his muscles move under his t-shirt and the sweat beads on the back of his neck. It was erotic in a weird sort of way. The act of exertion a form of submission. She would forgive him, Metta decided, but she liked the idea of making him work for it.

She finished her cigarette, stripped down to her bikini, and sauntered to the water's edge. She moved slowly and purposefully, and as gracefully as possible, to make sure her husband noticed. She stood for a moment, just long enough for him to take in her body, and then slid into the lake. The temperature was warm enough to make it feel like a bath and it soothed her skin. She relaxed and stretched out as she floated on the surface. Then she turned to face her husband.

"Aren't you joining me then?" She asked with mock indignation.

"Almost finished!" Christopher panted. Metta formed a wry smile in the corner of her mouth. She kicked out with both legs and propelled herself away from the shore.

"Don't be too long," she said with a purr, enjoying the sight of him frantically trying to complete his task. The poor boy wasn't the strongest swimmer and she knew she held all the power in this situation.

"Done!" He cried out and threw the inflatable onto the water. Heedless he leapt in after it, creating a wave which swamped Metta. She spluttered as the water covered her face and tried to stand so she could catch her breath, but the water was too deep here and she sank beneath the surface. Her body tensed as adrenaline flooded her system before she frantically kicked upwards. There was a moment of panic before she broke the surface and could taste clear air again. After a few spluttering coughs her rage had well and truly returned.

"Fucking Hell, Christopher!"

"Sorry, Metty. Are you alright?" Christopher began to paddle up to her, but she swam to keep the distance between them.

"No! The water's too deep and I don't need you piling more on top. I almost drowned."

"Oh shit, I'm sorry," he said, and Metta could tell he meant it. She looked away. She wasn't ready to forgive him and he was using his puppy dog eyes again. "Metta, I mean it. I didn't think. I'm sorry."

"Yeah? Well, you always seem to be apologising, don't you?" As she said it, she realised the words cut him more deeply that she had intended, but she couldn't take them back now. Christopher grabbed the inflatable and swam up to her.

"I'm sorry Metta. I've been a twat, haven't I?" His eyes searched hers and communicated so much: concern, worry, hurt, yet still retained some small trace of humour. In that moment they both came to the realisation that the spat was pointless.

"Yes you have," agreed Metta. "Completely."

"A complete twat, you're right," he nodded. "You're absolutely right, but give me a chance to make it up to you."

"What did you have in mind?" Metta sighed, but as she did so she couldn't help smiling.

"Well, you can have this for a start," he said as he leaned forward and kissed her. His lips were still hot but the kiss was gentle, and then he stroked some strands of hair from her cheek. She kissed him back, harder. Reaching around him, digging her nails into his back, she pulled him close. The kiss became more passionate and Metta soon felt him getting hard. The thrill of excitement was cut short however, as a child let out a piercing scream further down the beach, reminding them how close they were to civilisation. The moment passed and Metta broke away.

"Promise me you'll never infect me with one of those," she said.

"I promise," he said. "Now, let's do what we came here to do and relax." He grabbed the lilo and held it steady as Metta rolled on to it. He fetched her cigarettes, phone, headphones and sunglasses and soon she was relaxing and listening to her music.

Floating serenely Metta was finally able to let herself unwind a little. She felt very decadent, lazing in the sunshine, eyes closed, the music sending her off to her own little world. Metta imagined that she was in a private pool in her own mansion. No, she was in the bay on the edge of her own private island. Yeah, that was it. The light sea breeze and tropical fish swimming beneath her in crystal clear water. There was a distant murmur through the music as Christopher called out that he was heading back to the shop. He was off to buy a second inflatable and did she want anything? Metta shook her head. She had everything she wanted right here. Sun, cigarettes and Green Day. She smiled as she felt herself drifting on the water and the real world faded away.

As one of her favourite songs came on, *Wake Me Up When September Ends*, she imagined Billie Joe was singing it just for her. He was her one celebrity fantasy. In fact, Metta had been having sex fantasies about Billie Joe Armstrong for as long as she could remember having sex fantasies. Their relationship was a fully formed creation inside her mind, and it had been going on so long that it felt as genuine as most of the real relationships she'd had.

She imagined him entering the water and swimming up to her, stroking her hair and running his fingers over her body. His hands were light and cool against her hot skin. It brought her out in goosebumps. A smile rose to her lips and she shifted her weight as she crossed her legs. Wetness covered the back of her thighs, but it was cold and clammy.

What?

Metta opened her eyes as she snapped out of her reverie. Lake water had covered the surface of the inflatable and had begun to pool in the curves and dips caused by her body. Its chill felt unnatural and invasive, especially as it had seemed warm only a few moments before. Instinctively she sat up, but this only caused more water to flow over her. She scooped her hands and started bailing, annoyed at the interruption. Was it the result of a rogue wave, perhaps something passed by her.She looked around but couldn't see what caused it.

Then there was a sharp pull as her headphones were yanked from her ears. There was a moment of confusion before Metta had a terrible realisation and looked down to see her phone sinking into the depths. She reached and grabbed the headphones, but as she tried to pull them up they were yanked out of the socket - the phone was gone.

"Fuck!" She yelled, frustrated by the loss. She knew she had insurance, but she hated the inconvenience. Plus, there were photos from that morning that hadn't been backed up.

"Chris!" She called out, but Chris didn't answer. She searched for him, but then realised she had drifted out into the centre of the lake and the shore was far away.

Metta couldn't believe she was this far out, how she had not noticed the pull from the current? Then she remembered: Billie Joe, she'd been dreaming of Billie Joe. She could have been tied to a speed boat and probably wouldn't have noticed.

Metta couldn't believe she was so far out. A low mist hung over the surface of the water, which she assumed must be caused by some kind of atmospheric pressure drop over the now still water. Possibly the depth of the lake and the altitude of the mountain caused sudden changes in water temperature? However, it still unnerved her, how quickly the weather had turned. The air seemed different too, colder. It must be pretty deep out here and she realised there was no point attempting to dive down to retrieve her phone. The only thing she could do was swim back to shore.

Metta slid off the inflatable and into the lake. She let out a gasp as the chilling water hit her. It was almost a completely different body of water to the one she had entered. She pulled the lilo under her arms and chin as she kicked with her legs. Her skin stung with the cold, but she tried to push it from her mind. She looked to the shore and swam.

She could see the shop in the distance, but the people were too small and indistinguishable to see which one was her husband. It was unbelievable how far away they appeared, but then Metta remembered hearing something about how distance to the horizon isn't as far as it seems, or was it that it was further than it seems? Fuck it, she had no choice but to keep swimming.

She found herself getting annoyed at Chris. Why did he not shout when he saw her drifting out? He couldn't have spent all this time at the shop. She groaned inwardly as she imagined him trying to call her and wondering why it was going straight to voicemail.

She swam and swam, but the shore didn't seem to be getting any closer. She tried to work out how long she'd been on the inflatable with her eyes closed. She had listened to about three songs, so maybe ten or fifteen minutes? Even in a strong current it shouldn't take too long to get back to shore, but she didn't seem to be making any progress. Metta began to count to herself so she would have a rough concept of time. She counted to one hundred, but the distance stayed the same. She counted to two hundred, then three, but still the shore seemed as far away as ever.

Metta tried not to panic. She swam harder. Her heart thumped in her chest and sweat dripped down her face and stung her eyes. She swam until finally her legs were so tired that she had to straddle the inflatable to keep afloat.

She lay there for a while. It'll be okay, she told herself. If there is a strong current under the surface then it has to take me near land at some point. It's a mountain lake, so there would have to be a bottleneck somewhere. Maybe someone in a boat or on a jet-ski will come along and take me back to land? She felt embarrassed and stupid. How had she found herself in this situation?

Metta thought about Chris. She hoped he had noticed her absence by now and had raised an alarm. People would be looking for her. She would be okay. She closed her eyes and let the low lying mist wash over her. It had a faint odour that she couldn't quite place. It felt like she was in another world. It'll be okay, she told herself, everything would be okay. Slowly she became aware that she was sinking.

It was gradual, almost imperceptible but she was definitely becoming submerged. Her heart was in her throat and blood pulsed through her ears. She was too tired to swim anymore. Please, just stay afloat a little longer, let me rest, she pleaded. She squeezed the inflatable and sure enough, it was softer. Perhaps it had sprung a leak when she'd swam. She looked around to see if she was nearer the shore but it still looked far away.

"Chris!" She shouted. Tears ran down her face and her nose filled with fluid. Where was he? He was always so dependable. He was her rock. Always.

She couldn't explain why, but she felt betrayed by the fact he wasn't there. She shouted his name again, hoping to hear a response, but there was nothing. She looked around for something, anything, that could give her hope. The water was dark and foreboding. Then, for the briefest of moments, she thought she saw movement in the depths. Her blood turned cold. It's just a fish, she told herself. That's all it could be, but for some reason she felt she was being watched.

She shouted for help, for anyone to save her. She felt foolish, but she couldn't think of anything else to do. She clutched the inflatable, but it seemed to be deflating even faster now. The water was coming in from all sides and it was freezing. Something was happening, something unnatural. The mist was getting thicker around her and she knew by instinct that something was below her.

Her shouts turned to screams as the inflatable lilo that had been her lifeboat became a useless tangle of plastic around her limbs. Metta thrashed around in panic. No, not like this, she told herself. I will not die like this. She had a feeling that whatever was lurking under the surface would attack soon, so she let go of the lilo and attempted to swim for it. It might be hopeless, but she had to try. She swam with every ounce of energy she had. She would reach the shore and find her husband and he would hold her and she would hold him. They would never let each other go again.

She kicked and kicked but just couldn't disentangle the lilo from her right leg. It was wrapped round like a piece of seaweed. She knew she needed to free herself, but she couldn't waste a single moment's effort Then it pulled at her.

The lilo was actually tugging at her leg. Had it caught on something or was something pulling the other end? She tried to look behind her, but saw nothing but mist. Frantic, she reached down to untangle herself, but felt the pull again. Something had taken hold of the lilo.

She only had a split second, but she took a deep breath before her entire body was pulled under. She tried to make out what was tugging at her, but the water was dark and blurry. She could see the yellow streak of deflating plastic and a load of bubbles, but nothing past that. Adrenaline burned through her system. She looked back up to the surface and saw the glint of sunlight. She tried to swim upwards, to wrestle herself free but her limbs were leaden. Her lungs burned and she blew air through her nose to relieve some of the pressure. She wasn't going to last long, but she still clung to a feeling of hope. Not like this, Metta thought. It can't end like this.

The pull was even stronger and she was deep underwater now. She felt the water pressure build against her and realised there was no use fighting it anymore. As the last of her breath left her body, she sank into the darkness accepting her fate. Her lips trembled and burned and then finally she gulped and let the water rush in to fill her lungs.

And just in that final moment, when darkness and eternity embraced her, she felt the touch on the back of her hand.

It had her.

COFFEE AND CTHULHU

IAN MILLSTED

I was back in Bristol for the first time in seven years. Much of it looked unchanged. There were some new buildings on either side of the tracks as we eased in to Temple Meads station; signs of the investment the city had sought out so eagerly. But there was more dereliction too. Domestic buildings I remembered as being sought after places to live were now boarded up. At the back of one of the old rail sheds was a huge graffiti slogan 'Cthulhu is a wanker' below which, and to the same scale, was a picture of a phallus with several tentacles wrapped around it. My laughter died in my throat when I noticed the shocked looks of several of my fellow passengers. One woman tutted. I wondered if it was the graphic nature of the street art which bothered her or the challenge to the new orthodoxy. You could never be sure these days.

It took me a while to realise there was no evidence of anybody living on the streets. Around Paddington, where I'd walked just ninety minutes earlier, there were people huddled in sleeping bags or blankets on every corner, victims of the weakness of the so-called government. Here I saw none. I'd seen the spokesman for the mayor's office on screen make the bold claim that they had solved homelessness in the city but had been sceptical. If it was that easy wouldn't every city do the same? I'd heard other rumours too.

The walk to the Development Board building took me past the place where I remembered the St Nicholas church and market used to be. Both had been demolished and in their place stood a new skills training centre. Is this where the homeless people were? The lights were on inside and I could see tidy looking people sitting at tidy looking screen units.

I had enough time to stop for a coffee and gather my thoughts before the interview. Just an espresso. I was keen to get the job and Julie was even keener. She was desperate to get out of London. The room where we lived was too small for the two of us and soon there would be three. She was right. Our child should have a better future and the West Country was where the action was now.

Fortified by the caffeine, I made my way to the custom built offices in Castle Park. The building was imposing. The symbol of the Western Development Board was visible on all sides as I walked around to find the entrance. I'd read how that same insignia had once been a secret sign, known only to the select few who had the time and inclination to study arcane matters. The Oakfield incident had changed all that. Where many cities had resisted what was being offered from beyond, with rationalist deniers forming unlikely coalitions with religious groups against what the media dubbed the 'Great Old Ones'. Bristol had been different. The transition to an economic climate favourable to new energy sources and investment had been smooth and rapid. I wondered how much of that way of thinking had been in place before Oakfield. Opponents called it Cthulhu Economics, but the effect was quantifiable. Bristol had become a boom city.

The receptionist sent me straight on up to the fifth floor. One other person, another interviewee was already sat on the sofa seat. I made the usual pleasantries as we waited. She was a post doc at Miskatonic and qualified for the post. This wasn't going to be easy. Nor was it just the two of us. A few minutes after my arrival a third person joined us. She was from Brichester; almost local. She seemed flustered, possibly worried that she was slightly late and that might go against her. As she leant forward to check she had everything in her bag, I noticed that she wore a crucifix on a chain around her neck. She spotted my glance and pushed it back inside her blouse, which she buttoned up closer to the neck. I looked away, feigning disinterest.

The three of us were separated for most of the rest of the morning as we completed a carousel of tasks. Lunch was one of those necessarily false affairs where we all tried to appear interested to hear about each other's families and backgrounds, all the while knowing that only one of us would be successful and the likelihood would be that we would never see each other again.

It was in the afternoon that things became less predictable. I was led to a small, spartan conference room which contained two people I had not previously seen. Each had a screen on their laps. The only other thing in the room was an empty chair to which one of them gestured. I sat. There were no introductions. The younger of the two spoke first. "What," he asked, "makes you think you're more suitable for the position than either of the other candidates?" I paused. Was this a test? Was the girl with the crucifix a plant? I pointed out my skills and experiences and what I could bring to the job. I had barely started when the older man interrupted me. "Yes, yes, we have all that already. What we are asking is why you think you should be appointed and not the other candidates?" Clearly I was being tested. I replied that I had no connections to any organisation that opposed the presence of the new benefactors. The older man smiled and nodded. "Quite so," he said. "Good."

The younger man passed his screen across to the older man and pointed to something I could not see. The older man just said, "yes". The younger man started to speak to me again.

"We have long term investments in the Brichester area. Here is a mail we have written to your rival candidate's present employers." He paused a little after he said the word 'present'. "As you will see it gives them a little advice about their employee that they may wish to know. We would like you to put your name to it and send it for us. This would be your first action as our new director of research." He passed me the screen. "Of course," he continued, "you may feel this is not your concern, in which case we expect our friend from Miskatonic University will be able to help us."

I took the screen. I added my name to the sign off at the end of the message and sent it.

"Welcome to the company," the older man said.

I barely registered the flurry of activity that followed. I was shown to another room where I was given various documents to take away, read and sign. Eventually I returned to the station. I stopped at the same coffee shop so that I could phone Julie to give her the good news. While we talked, I saw the woman from Brichester through the window. She was on the other side of the street searching in her pocket for something. She drew out her phone and started talking. She looked shocked by whatever she was hearing. I realised I knew. The coffee I was drinking reminded me where I was, who I was, what I was doing. Sickened by what I had done I went to the toilets in the coffee shop and threw up. I must have been loud as one of the baristas popped in to see if I was okay. I splashed water on my face and left.

I decided not to take the direct way back to the station but walked along some side roads to see if a place I remembered from my teenage years was still there. It was. I found what I was looking for.

The sky was turning darker but I felt a greater purpose with the cans of spray paint now resting in my bag. I phoned Julie to tell her I might be later back than I had thought.

A PIECE OF THE PUZZLE

CHERYL MORGAN

Sonia Greene read through the newspaper advertisement again, tapping her pen against her lips. Then, decision made, she fetched some sheets of notepaper from her stationery drawer and began to write.

Dear Howard...

It was important not to seem too forward. She had only known Howard a few months. They had met at an amateur press conference in Boston earlier in the year. He came from an old New England family and had been raised by his mother and aunts, so he had some fairly firm views about propriety. He had some other firm views as well, not all of them admirable, but he had a lively mind and Sonia was sure that after a few years in New York he would develop a more balanced view of the world. And if he didn't, well, after Samuel Greene, she felt that she could put up with anything. Howard wasn't going to beat her, so whatever else he did he would have to be an improvement.

Of course it would be better if she didn't need a husband but, despite all of the advances made by the suffragists it was still hard for a woman, especially a woman with a child, to make her own way in life without a man by her side. Her employers and colleagues at the department store had been very understanding. Fortunately she was a widow, not the divorcee she had feared she would have to become. Samuel's violent tendencies had finally turned against him, and he had killed himself rather than her or Florence. Thank goodness for the depressive state alcohol brings. And thank goodness it had happened when it did. Heaven only knew what furies Samuel would have got into had he lived to see a world in which the sale of alcohol was banned.

Still, Sonia had ambitions. Her job at the store was well paid, and allowed her to travel, but it was still a job. The store owned her. She created all sorts of fabulous hats for them, some of which were extremely popular, and all she got was a salary. Getting time off to go to amateur press conferences was difficult. And some of her best designs had been turned down because her bosses felt they were too adventurous for the general public. Sonia had seen similar things on sale for ridiculous prices at private millinery shops. No, she would start her own business as soon as she had all her plans in place. And sadly, even in this day and age, those plans had to include getting a husband.

Howard was no businessman, that much was clear, but it didn't matter. Sonia had been in enough business meetings to know how it went. The men were in charge, and another man, no matter how clueless about the issue in hand, would be listened to in a way that a woman would not. To start her own business she would have to talk to banks, rent a shop, and so on. Howard spoke well, and believed in being smartly dressed, even if he could not afford a decent quality suit. She could fix that. And with someone like him by her side, the process of starting a business would go much more smoothly.

Besides, there was the other thing; the writing. It was a love they both shared. Howard was good. No, he was very good. He might not have made any commercial sales yet, but it was bound to happen sooner or later. His work sent chills up her spine the way few other writers did. And, most importantly, he didn't laugh at her feeble efforts. She could publish amateur magazines all she wanted, and *The Rainbow* was getting a very favorable reception, but it wasn't the same thing as being a writer yourself. Howard had been kind about her work. He had encouraged her, said she had talent. For that she could forgive him a great deal.

What was that phrase again? Aisle, altar, hymn. Yes, get him away from those stuffy aunts, stop him moping over the death of his mother (which, from the sound of it, had been a mercy for the woman), get him to spend more time with her friends at the Blue Pencil Club, and she'd soon have him grow out of his old-fashioned

Providence attitudes. New York was the place to be. Everything and everyone came here.

Take Alice Bailey, for example. She was a leading British occultist from London; someone who could just pop in and out of the British Museum every day to do research. How Howard would envy that. And yet she was coming here to New York to give a series of lectures on; Science and Consciousness'. It was just the sort of thing that Howard loved. Other members of the Blue Pencil Club would likely want to attend as well. It was an ideal opportunity.

How, then, to work this? Howard couldn't stay at her apartment. That would not be proper. Besides, Florence might come home, and then there would be a row. Sonia could not understand it. Had she been that sulky and difficult as a teenager? No, she had not. She had been grateful for all the hard work her mother had undertaken to establish a new life in America after the death of Sonia's father. Sonia's step-father had been a decent, hard-working man too, but mainly it was down to being a Good Jewish Mother and looking after your family whatever it took. How could Florence not see that?

The ungrateful child spent more of her time out of the home than in it. She skipped school, spent her evenings at flapper parties dancing to jazz (Howard would *not* approve – darkie music), and insisted on calling herself Carol because Florence was '… old fashioned and horrible, how could you have been so cruel as to have called me *that*, Mother?' Well, if the girl went and got herself pregnant, she'd just have to marry whichever boy it had been that week, and then she'd be off Sonia's hands. It was a tragedy, but there it was. There was only so much a mother could do.

So no, Howard could not stay here. And he would probably not want to stay with someone else in the Blue Pencil Club because he didn't know them that well yet and would not want to be indebted to a stranger. She'd have him round for dinner one evening and feed him, because God knows he was in need of feeding – those aunts of his clearly had no idea how to cook – but he would have to stay in a hotel. Sonia could afford that. The problem was how to suggest it to Howard in such a way that he would not feel he was receiving charity…

***

Sat in a bar with her friends after the second lecture, Sonia had to admit that it was all going very well. Alice Bailey was a strange woman, and she had some very odd ideas, but she presented them in a compelling manner that had the men sitting up and taking notice of what she said. Sonia, if she was honest with herself, was more interested in how Bailey was managing to hold the crowd's attention than in what she said. Howard, however, was fascinated. Quite a few of the Blue Pencil Club, including Reinhardt Kleiner and James Morton, had come along and Sam Loveman had come all the way from Chicago to hear Bailey talk.

Loveman was an invert, Sonia was sure of that. Howard wouldn't approve if he knew, but he was even more socially clueless than most men. Women could tell, though. An invert would treat you as a human being, not just consider whether he wanted to sleep with you or not. At first Sonia had suspected that Howard might be an invert. That was before she worked out that he was just painfully shy and socially awkward. Loveman had been a protégé of Ambrose Bierce. He was in the middle of a project to translate Baudelaire and Verlaine into English. He was a real literary person. That meant a lot to Howard.

Thanks to Bailey's fascinating lecture, conversation was flowing freely. It would have been better with a nice glass of red wine, Sonia thought, but at least Prohibition was forcing New York bars to up the quality of the coffee they served in order to keep customers. The men were discussing one of the ideas Bailey had put forward in her lecture.

'We might extend the idea still further and consider a planet as an atom. Perhaps there is a life within the planet that holds the substance of the sphere and all forms of life upon it to itself as a coherent whole, and that has a specific extent of influence. This may sound like a wild speculation yet, judging from analogy, there may perhaps be within the planetary sphere an Entity Whose consciousness is as far removed from that of man as the consciousness of man is from that of the atom of chemistry.'

Kleiner dismissed this as fanciful. If such an Entity existed, he asked, why had we seen no evidence of it? Why had it not spoken to us? Howard was more taken with the idea.

"Why would it care?" he asked. "What would we be to it? Consider an ant hill. It is full of living beings. They must have intelligence, for they are able to build homes in which to live, and cooperate with each other to fetch food and raise their young. Yet to us they are a mere nuisance. We destroy a nest of ants without a thought for what their civilization has produced. They may see us, but we don't talk to them because they are as nothing to us. How much more uncaring, therefore, would a being be who is as far above us as we are above the atom?"

"That's scary, Howard." Sonia could sense he was working on a story idea.

"It is horrific beyond imagining. We modern folk are used to living in a world defined by science. The stars and planets move in their courses according to the mathematics of Newton and Einstein. What Mrs Bailey has suggested is that there might be Entities in the universe to Whom stars are mere playthings. They might, at any time, choose to snuff ours out. And They would neither know nor care that we would be wiped out as a result."

"But surely, Howard," scoffed Morton, waving his cigar with disdain, "surely this is all just Mrs Bailey re-using the old alchemical idea of 'As Above, So Below'. It is mysticism, pure and simple, not something that men of science should be concerned about."

Morton was something of a Socialist. He campaigned for civil rights for the blacks. Politically he and Howard could not be further apart, and they were always arguing over something. Sonia could not understand why they were becoming good friends. Still, she was indebted to Morton for having introduced her to Howard, and their arguments tended to be highly entertaining. Before Howard could respond, however, Sam Loveman intervened.

"Don't be so quick to dismiss alchemy, Jim. Hasn't Professor Rutherford proved that one element can be changed into another?"

"Well yes, but only in a university laboratory, with fantastically complicated equipment. Not by waving his hands over a bubbling pot of potions and muttering mumbo-jumbo." Morton demonstrated by trying to transmute his coffee into gold, but succeeded only in waving cigar ash everywhere.

Sam protected his coffee with his hat. "That's true, but who knows what might be possible. If we were having this conversation ten years ago, none of us would have heard of Einstein or Rutherford, and our view of what is scientifically possible would be very different."

"I'll believe in magic when I see it with my own eyes. But I suppose, Sam, that you are going to tell us you *have* seen such things."

Loveman was quiet for a while, and then said, with all seriousness, "Actually, Jim, I am. A couple of months ago in Chicago I saw a magic show by an Egyptian guy with an unpronounceable name. Nyer-Fotep or something like that. You know me – Jim, Howard, Reinhardt – I'm as skeptical as they come. But what this guy did was astonishing. And I'm here, in New York, yes to see Alice Bailey, but also because I've been told that this guy will do a show here. It's Wednesday night. I have the details here somewhere."

Sam rummaged in his pocket and pulled out a crumpled flier which he smoothed out and passed to Howard.

"The Great Nyarlathotep, Master of the Magic of the Pharaohs," read Howard, pronouncing the name without difficulty. "Well it is very flattering of him, but you've obviously been taken in by a charlatan."

"I have?"

Howard looked a little crestfallen, so Sonia jumped into the conversation.

"Yes Sam, don't you remember? Howard had a story in *The United Amateur* last year. It was called 'Nyarlathotep', and it was about an Egyptian magician."

"Well, darn it, you are right! It had totally slipped my mind. But now you mention it, Sonia, *of course* I remember it. It was a fine piece of work, Howard. And yet... I did go to that show in Chicago. I can't remember all the details, but I remember being very impressed by what I saw, and frankly deeply disturbed that anyone could have that level of power over nature."

"Are you sure you haven't been eating peyote with the Navajo, Sam?" asked Morton jovially, slapping Loveman on the back and causing him to splutter coffee over the table.

"Sam's as honest a fellow as I know," said Howard, generously. "Besides, he has brought this theft of my work to my attention. We must attend this event on Wednesday, Sam, and confront this foreign devil with his appropriation of my story. I won't stand for it. Sonia, where is this Hanley place?"

Sonia took the flier from Howard and glanced at the address.

"P.J. Hanley's Bar. On Court and Nelson. That's just on the edge of Red Hook, which isn't the nicest part of Brooklyn, but it is safe enough."

"I know the place," said Morton. "It's run by an Irishman called Jack Ryan. Rumor has it that it is a speakeasy. Is that why you want to go there, Sam?"

"Well I could certainly have done with a whiskey or two after seeing Nyar-wotsit's show the first time around," said Loveman,

"I have never tasted intoxicating liquor, and never intend to," said Howard, primly. "Besides, I must be in full possession of my faculties in order to confront this imposter."

"That's a show I'd much rather see than a bunch of magic tricks," said Kleiner. "Sadly James and I already have an engagement for Wednesday night. Do enjoy yourselves, gentlemen, and don't forget to tell us all about it when we next see you."

**

The clientele of P.J. Hanley's turned out to be largely blond seamen, that part of New York being the Norwegian ghetto. This was a great relief to Sonia, who had worried that there might be a lot of darkies and that Howard would go off on one of his rants. Norwegians he approved of, though of course he was still in high dudgeon over the magician having stolen his stage name from that story.

The bar was indeed a speakeasy. Sonia and Howard drank ginger beer, which she was fairly sure was non-alcoholic though one could never be quite sure. Alcohol was only served in a back room that could not be seen from the streets. The show was apparently taking place in a cellar accessible only via a steep set of stairs from that room.

Descending the stairs, Sonia, Howard and Sam found themselves in a room much larger than they had anticipated. Indeed, it was much larger than Sonia felt ought to exist under an unassuming part of Brooklyn. Even more strangely, there were other entrances. Down the stairs from Hanley's came a throng of Norwegians, now even more quiet and morose than normal for intoxicated Scandinavians. Other doorways disgorged various groups of working men, all of them apparently a little drunk yet unusually silent. It was as if every speakeasy in Brooklyn had a staircase leading into the same vast underground auditorium. There must have been at least five hundred men gathered there. Sonia was acutely aware that she appeared to be the only woman.

They took their seats, and the man calling himself Nyarlathotep came on stage soon after. Howard was outraged to discover he was not in fact an Arab, but very dark skinned with a long, thin face. Sonia remembered meeting a man from Ethiopia with similar features. There was an argument between Sam and Howard as to whether the Nubian dynasty of Egypt counted as true Pharaohs or not. Howard held that the true Egyptians were white men, on account of their level of civilization, and that the current Arab population of the country was made up of degenerates resulting from inbreeding between true Egyptians and Africans.

Thankfully the show began quickly. Somewhat to Sonia's surprise, it started with a movie, though to her chagrin there was no sign of Douglas Fairbanks. Instead Nyarlathotep treated them to a film he claimed to have been shot in the sunken Egyptian port of Heracleion, and in other, far more ancient, drowned cities. The camera work seemed poor because the shapes of the buildings were all subtly off, as if there was something very wrong about their geometry.

Then the film changed. There were strange, futuristic scenes of war. Frightening mechanical fighting machines spewed death across a battlefield; aircraft dropped bombs that engulfed whole cities in flame; emaciated families were herded into trains and taken to camps where they were locked into rooms and died horribly from some unseen agent. There was a brief moment when a bright light obscured everything, and the screen showed nothing but a mushroom-shaped cloud of smoke. Africans lay dying of hunger as flies crawled over their scrawny bodies. Vast floods drowned futuristic coastal cities. A terrible plague filled cities with millions of corpses. The mushroom cloud returned.

When the film ended, Nyarlathotep returned to the stage and spoke.

"That, puny humans, was a small taste of the horrors that await in your future."

To Sonia's eyes, the magician seemed to expand in size until he dominated the auditorium; until he was snarling directly into her face. Like a rabbit staring into the eyes of a wolf, she kept perfectly still, desperately hoping he wouldn't notice that she was breathing.

"Some of you here have wondered what place man has in the vast, uncaring cosmos. For the most part, very little. You live, you breed, you die. In the eyes of the gods you are small, indistinguishable, replaceable. Yet every once in a while your species produces a mind so warped, so focused in its corruption, that it has the power to speak to millions down the centuries. I have called such a mind to me tonight so that it might serve me. A few of you have roles to play in the life of that mind. The rest of you pitiful creatures are nothing to me, but you will serve as food for my servants."

Through the doors of the auditorium oozed strange, jelly-like creatures covered in black slime and with dozens of eyes that darted back and forth ceaselessly. They appeared to have no mouths, but nevertheless they made a constant chuckling sound: "Tekeli-li, Tekeli-li". Above them, below a vaulted ceiling that could not possibly exist, hung black, faceless humanoid creatures, airborne on silent, leathery wings.

Sonia wanted to scream; she wanted to run, but her body would not obey her panicked mind. It was as much as she could do to glance across to Howard and Sam, who appeared as paralyzed as she was. She was gripped from behind by clawed hands and hauled upwards from her seat. She could see that the winged creatures had done the same to Howard and Sam.

Below them, the working men in the audience were released from Nyarlathotep's spell. They began to scream and fight with one another. Desperately, they formed a human pyramid in the center of the auditorium, each man fighting to get to the top. The Shoggoths herded them, flowing over the stragglers, the fallen, and consuming them. Those at the top hoped against hope that the creatures would satiate themselves on the weaker men. Or, if all else failed, they would at least have a few minutes more of life; be the last to be eaten.

Above the slaughter, the Nightgaunts' nimble, clawed fingers began their work. Though they held their victims fast, they were still able to wriggle, to tickle. Sonia looked down upon the panicked, screaming men, on the implacable, insatiable Shoggoths, and under the insistent ministrations of the Nightgaunts she laughed and laughed and laughed.

***

The following morning Sonia's apartment was draped in a fog of embarrassment. Neither she nor Howard, it seemed, could remember how or when they had returned there. All she could remember of the evening was visiting a speakeasy with Loveman. Someone must have spiked their drinks. Sonia concluded, sadly, that if you made the sale of alcohol illegal then the people who sold it would soon start behaving like criminals.

What she could remember, and presumably Howard did too, was the sex. They had gone at it like teenagers, like they were the last man and woman on the planet, desperate to ensure the continuation of the human race. It had been the best sex Sonia had ever had. For Howard it had probably been the first, but he clearly didn't want to talk about it and Sonia wasn't going to risk everything by pressing him.

He would leave today, go back to Providence. She knew that. He was too mortified by what they had done to do anything else. But the die was cast. In a few months time he would ask her to marry him. His sense of honour would allow nothing less.

***

Back home in Providence, Howard slept badly. After many nights of confusion he finally woke up in a cold sweat with the memory of a dream clear in his mind. He wrote a letter to Reinhardt Kleiner describing it. In the dream, he had received a letter from Sam Loveman, urging him to go to see a magician called Nyarlathotep. Howard suspected he had been having this dream for some time, and that it had somehow inspired his story of the same name, even though this was the first time he had remembered it.

***

In his palace in drowned R'lyeh, dread Cthulhu lay dreaming. He would not wake until the stars were right. But in that brief moment, in less time even than it took for the planet to once orbit its star, another piece of that vast, cosmic puzzle had fallen into place.

In his dreams, Cthulhu smiled.

HILLRAISER

KEN SHINN

A lot of people have the image of a demon as a big, ugly, sulphurous monster - all horns, fangs, red scaly skin and pants-shitting terror. And, sometimes, they're right. But demons, strictly speaking, are spirits. They can look however they choose to – read your Marlowe – and will often appear as something, or somebody, much more innocuous than they truly are.

That's very important. Remember that.

A lot of people have also got the idea that a demon is a relentlessly vicious and violent being, hell-bent(ha!) on causing torture, dismemberment, red-hot pokers up the fundament and eternal, agonising death/resurrection/death to hapless human victims. And, sometimes, they're right. But demons, strictly speaking, are creatures of mischief. They tend, on the whole, to be keener on the idea of anarchy, of *misrule*, rather than violent death *per se*.

That's also very important. Remember that.

And that same lot of people have also got it into their heads that a demon is somehow, inevitably, an anti-Christian creature, and, being such, will ensure that any deal that a human makes with it will be a hollow, meaningless thing, leading only to the aforementioned agonising death/resurrection/death routine. And, I have to be honest, sometimes, again, they're right. But demons, strictly speaking, are far from purely anti-Christian entities. Bone up on your myths and legends a bit, and you'll find demons everywhere, in every pantheon. And, if you play your cards right, then a deal made with a demon can be a very productive thing. Unlike, say, a Djinn, which will simply agree to wishes and then ensure that they go wrong, it is possible to strike a bargain with a demon which will end without being dragged off to the underworld for all eternity, as long as the *emptor* ensures that they've accounted for the appropriate *caveat*s.

And that is *particularly* important, so remember that, as well.

Anyway, with all of that in mind...

This all started when I decided to make a deal with a demon. It all seemed a relatively straightforward idea: I'd looked long and hard at the world around me, and decided that I deserved a much better place in it. The usual sort of things: recognition, wealth. If so many non-entities had managed that, then someone like me warranted at least as much. Why should so many ugly reality TV zombies and plastic-titted vacuities be better off than me? Now there's a *real* sin for you. Having no wish to follow in their inane footsteps, nor being any happier with the idea of driving a desk to infirmity and beyond in some mind-numbingly tedious office job, I realised that, being better than that, I could use my superior brainpower to end up where I really wanted to be.

That still left various ways to choose from. Become a famous footballer? No. I'm in good shape, physically, but I'm also sharp enough mentally not to want to kick a bladder brainlessly back and forth to get my due. Also, I'd need to have started as a school kid. Bit late for that. How about a famous novelist? Realistically, that was a no-no, as well. I know that I can write a damn sight better than a lot of the doorstop hacks, but breaking into the big league of writers is as much a matter of ridiculous luck as anything else, and I couldn't count on that. For the same reason, I wasn't too struck by the idea of becoming a pop sensation, or making my fortune by playing poker or gambling on the nags. I needed something with a clear set of rules, and a guaranteed return. Which only left one realistic option: striking a deal with the dark powers.

I won't go into the full details of how I summoned the demon involved. They were decidedly polytheistic and aimed at invoking a minor and relatively harmless entity. Dark cellar, candles, and more magical/religious paraphernalia than you can take. A mix of the arcane and the faintly ridiculous, with an undercurrent of menace. The proper stuff.

The anticipated swirls of eldritch smoke gradually coalesced into solid form. I wasn't quite sure what I'd expected, but it certainly wasn't the unassuming shape of a chubby, middle-aged man with the face of a bewildered cherub and thinning fair hair, nor for the preceding smoke to smell rather less like sulphur, and rather more like – yes, that was it – *egg custard*. He was dressed in what had once been a very sharp-looking suit, reduced by who knew how many years into a crumpled, slightly frayed state of comfort, rather than elegance. For some reason, he had an otter perched on one shoulder. And he looked very familiar. Where had I seen that face before? Oh, good grief. Surely it wasn't...

"Benny Hill?"

The man grinned at me. "At your service." He crossed his eyes and saluted me, with a cheery, idiotic smile. "And this is my otter." He gestured at the animal. "You're probably wondering why I've got an otter. See, we demons work best with a familiar, and the chaps in charge, they said to me, 'Well, it's always one thing or an otter.' I didn't like the sound of one thing – I've always preferred 'em in twos." His smile became a leer. The otter giggled – could otters giggle? – and scuttled down Hill's torso, disappearing down the front of his trousers. "There we are – the beast's back in his cage!"

I couldn't help but ask. "How did you end up as a demon? And why are you the demon that I should be dealing with?"

Hill's reply was swift and easy. "Well, sir, demons aren't always evil. We've got all sorts of things to do in the Universe, and some of 'em are even good things. I'm a demon of frivolity. It's my job to bring fun into the world, and from what we could work out, it's fun that you're looking for!"

In for a penny, I thought. "Well, in that case, I think that we can make a deal, Benny! Let's get down to business" – Hill sniggered dirtily – "and sort out this contract, shall we?"

I won't go into the contract at great length – I'd read up all of the legal stuff carefully. In brief, what I wanted was wealth for the rest of my natural life, and recognition as well. I was careful about that 'natural life,' ensuring that I wouldn't die in an accident, a murder, or from illness – only from ripe old age – and that, if I had a soul, it would not be forfeit. That was obviously a lot to ask for, but I had the perfect bargain to offer Hill.

"If you can give me that, then I'll stipulate that you be released into my world, *for as long as you wish*. Once you go back to the

Great Beyond, you stay there: but you only go back when you want to. How about that, eh?"

Hill looked thoughtful, disappeared in a puff of egg custard fumes, and returned three minutes later with a big grin and a contract. I read it thoroughly, smiled myself, and signed it.

And thus began the series of events which have led me to my present pass. Sitting in a cheap hotel room in Istanbul, richer than Croesus, recognised *everywhere* that I go, and wishing desperately that I'd just decided to be a civil servant instead.

I'd asked one more thing of Hill – that he call in on me each day before I went to bed, just to check on how he was doing, whether he was ready to go back, that sort of thing. He agreed to this happily enough, and advised me to check my bank account. "You'll be pleasantly surprised," he chuckled, and walked out of my flat.

So I did just that. To my delight, the ATM showed a balance of one million pounds credit. I decided to celebrate by taking out my maximum daily allowance of three hundred. That would be more than enough to tide me over for the day – I could entertain myself with bigger purchases tomorrow.

I was on my way to the local pub, visions of Bollinger dancing in my head, when I saw Hill strolling down the road a short distance ahead. Workers, shoppers, and general pedestrians paid him no heed. The sun shone on a beautiful day. A policeman patrolled calmly down the pavement towards Hill.

And then Hill turned abruptly into a near-invisible waft of smoke, and vanished directly into the ear of a passer-by. The man froze for a moment, then reached inside his coat, produced a large custard pie, and slammed it directly into the cop's face.

There was a moment of quiet. Then, as the riled cop wiped cream from his eyes, a loud, brassy tune blared out of the air all around. A jaunty, cheerily mindless tune that I recognised at once.

The policeman grabbed at the man's collar, but somehow missed. His grip caught the dress of an attractive young woman walking by, and somehow tore it off – with a loud, cartoonish rip – in one go. Underneath, she was wearing only a skimpy bra and panties, suspenders and stockings, and high heels. She screamed in outrage, and aimed a surprisingly powerful punch at the cop, who sailed backwards into a greengrocer's display, cascading apples, oranges and bananas all over the pavement. More pedestrians slipped on these, executing painful-looking involuntary pratfalls.

The chaos swirled for several more moments. Everyone was loudly blaming each other, until the cop suddenly bellowed "OI!", and pointed a trembling finger at the nearby figure of the instigator, who was at that moment grinning broadly as he slapped a little bald man sharply around the head.

The sight immediately galvanised the crowd into a purposeful mob. With fury in their faces and much waving of fists, they ran towards the man. A comical look of dismay crossed his face, and he promptly took off in an odd, pixilated sprint: and, at the same instant, the pace of his pursuers took on the same strange, jerky quality. However bizarre it looked, they all moved at a very high speed. I followed as best as I could, determined to see what ensued.

What ensued was havoc. The chase grew as it went on: innocent passers-by were clouted, groped, or soaked, and joined the pursuit. Windows were broken, cars swerved and collided, shops were left in ruin as the stampede raced in and out of each one. What had started as a moment of slapstick had fast become a full-scale riot. My initial surprised amusement had become bewildered dismay.

I followed in its wake, trying my best to keep the mob's quarry in sight. At a crucial moment, as they were distracted by bickering among themselves, he slipped around a corner and out of sight.

In an instant, everything returned to normal. Shop windows were whole again: clothing returned to bodies, undamaged; pavements were clear of debris. It was as though none of the preceding few minutes had happened. The man appeared back around the corner. He shook his head briskly, and carried on his way as before. So did every other member of the erstwhile mob. But there was a difference. Where, before, they'd just been going on their way, they were all now doing so with a spring in their step and a smile on their face. The whole mood of the scene had become suddenly *happy*.

A wisp of smoke rushed past my head, behind a wall – and, seconds later, Hill appeared from behind it, his grin broader than ever, and going quietly on his way. He walked to a nearby bus stop. I knew that the next bus wasn't due for another ten minutes, and had a brainwave. It took me five minutes to hire the taxi and lie in wait. When Hill boarded the bus for the city centre, I told the cabbie to follow.

Hill got off by the city hall. I managed to disembark quickly by paying the driver fifty quid for a ten-pound journey and telling him to keep the change. As Hill strolled past a stern-looking female functionary and her junior colleague, an otter emerged from the back of his trousers and nipped the woman smartly on the arse.

As she wheeled round gaping, Hill once more turned into that vague puff of vapour and blew into the man's ear on a non-existent breeze. Again, that crazed music blasted out of the still air. The woman hurled the contents of the coffee cup that she'd been carrying straight into the bespectacled youth's face.

And the jerky, high-speed chase began once more, with ever-increasing numbers of innocent bystanders dragged into its Hamelin-like havoc. As before, the damage to both property and people appeared to be horrendous. As before, the frantic quarry at last managed to disappear from the mob's view for a moment. As before, the whole situation immediately resolved itself, leaving the route of the chase as unharmed as before and the hunters cheery and chipper. And as before, that waft of smoke whizzed by, and Hill appeared and wandered off looking pleased.

I shadowed him discreetly for another couple of hours, and saw the same phenomenon several more times. Finally, as the afternoon turned into early evening, I found myself in the pub that I'd initially been looking for, ordered the best champagne in the bar as a starter, and pondered on what I'd seen.

So, Hill – a demon – was loosed upon the World for as long as he likes, to do whatever he likes, with certain constraints. He goes forth and – presumably for his personal amusement or some need for routine mischief – pours his spirit into some random individual's ear and causes chaos to ensue, at the end of which everyone seems a lot more content with Life. He's a demon, but he appears to be doing some sort of good. And he's doing it by briefly possessing human hosts to act as a catalyst.

The pun occurred to me as I was finishing my second glass, and I was rather proud of it.

Hill is other people.

I made my way home that night half-cut and thoughtful. I was looking forward to seeing Hill, and had some questions to ask him. I felt that he'd largely be confirming my theories, but there was a sense of anticipation in that for me as well. When he finally appeared in my lounge, I offered him a large Chivas Regal and a Sobranie, and bade him sit, which he did. His otter curled up comfortably on his lap. My queries were simple: did he want to return to the Netherworld yet, and what had he been up to that day?

Hill's replies were equally straightforward: a thoughtful "no" to the first, and to the second, a comment that "I've been spreading a little happiness." Both he and the otter giggled at that. Frankly, that was good enough for me. I bade them both a good night, and they promptly disappeared with a smell of baked confectionery. And I was left with a definite feeling of envious curiosity. What must it be like to be able to cause such havoc, *and get away with it?*

After a good night's sleep, I awoke and decided to take advantage of another sunny day. Hill was nowhere to be seen, but that didn't matter – I'd see him later. I decided to take out another three hundred quid, just because I could, and was mildly surprised to find out that my balance still read one million pounds. Maybe a delay in showing the transaction? No big problem. That day, having arranged a suitable line of credit, I treated myself to a new, high-quality laptop and a crate of Talisker, picked up some holiday brochures for various countries that I'd always wanted to visit, and rounded off the day by buying some recently-released books that I'd been after and enjoying another drunken night down my local.

I was taken aback when Hill appeared for our nightly meeting. He was wearing black trousers, a striped shirt, and a beret, clutching a bottle of wine. His otter lolled at his feet, a string of onions around its neck, puffing contentedly away on what looked very like a Gauloise. He gave the same answers to my questions. When I went on to ask him why he was so clad, he reasserted that he was just spreading happiness. I humoured him with a huge, Gallic shrug and a "C'est la vie."

"Lavvy," Hill riposted with a chortle, before he and his otter disappeared once more. Before I slept that night, I was brooding over this puzzle. I was also wondering why I wasn't being recognised yet, as I'd asked. Money I had, yes, but did people know me? It was early days, but I had expected something more immediate. I finally decided on what I needed to look for when I next saw Hill. Feeling more settled having done this, I got my head down.

The next morning, my first action was to check my bank account both online and at my nearest branch. Despite my withdrawals and my credit purchases showing clearly, both checks put the balance at a steady one million pounds. I decided to go for a very large fry-up. As I was finishing mopping my plate and preparing to order a refill on my coffee, it all became clear. When Hill had been an earthly creature, being a millionaire was recognised generally as being *extremely* rich. It still wasn't exactly common now, but a million was generally recognised as a level of considerable, not exceptional, wealth. Hill doubtless reasoned that, if I always had a million pounds – no more, no less – to my name, then I'd be a very wealthy man. He was ensuring that I'd *always* be a millionaire because that was how *he* judged vast amounts of money. I felt pleased to have figured that out. I was beginning to understand how Hill worked.

And with hindsight, I should've held that over-confidence firmly in check.

That evening, Hill reappeared clad in khaki shorts and safari jacket, with a bush hat a-dangle with corks, holding a boomerang. Meanwhile, his otter supped noisily from a tube of Foster's. We exchanged our usual words – no change – they disappeared... and I added a new piece of information to my theories. Hill was travelling the world, and playing out the chase in the process. And it all seemed increasingly fun to me – misrule with impunity. Tomorrow night, I decided, I'd ask Hill for a little favour. He still owed me, after all.

The day passed quietly. As I sprawled in my armchair and lit another fag, Hill appeared. I wasted no time on my request. "Look, Benny – I know that I have the money, but people aren't exactly double-taking in the streets, are they? I asked for recognition as well as wealth, remember?"

Hill looked shamefaced. I pressed home my advantage. "I understand that it might not be immediate, but it is still a potential breach of contract. So here's my offer. I'm prepared for it to take, say, another week – but I want a favour in return. I know what you've been doing. And I want to try it myself. The next time that you do your business, I want you to let me lead the chase."

Hill sucked his teeth noisily like a dodgy mechanic. "Lead it? Well, if that's what you want. But you need to realise that it could be a bit odd for you. The people that I steer around aren't aware that I'm responsible. Our deal *links* me to you. You'd be aware that I was influencing events. You'd feel me inside your head. Would you be comfortable with that?"

"Yes," I replied without hesitation. I wasn't missing out on an opportunity like this. Chaos without consequences! "Just one thing. Let me get a good night's kip and some breakfast before we start. And make sure that your otter cleans up before he goes to bed." The creature in question had its paws wrapped around a bottle of ouzo this time, and was on its back swigging away. Hill chuckled. "Don't worry – I'll see that he's tucked up all snug with his otter water bottle. You just get that sleep. You'll need it."

The next morning, after a large plate of bacon and eggs, a shave, a wash, and dressing in a T-shirt and some combat fatigues, I was ready to go. The sunny weather still held out as Hill and I made our way to a suitably crowded street for the start of the fun. I could already feel adrenaline stirring in my system.

Hill looked me in the eye with mock-solemnity. "Are you still sure that you want to do this? Last chance to say different... "

I grinned back at him. "Let's do it."

Hill shifted into his smoky spirit form, and rushed into my ear. I'd once had wax syringed from my ears, and the odd, inrushing sensation felt very similar. I blinked rapidly several times, feeling slightly disorientated.

When I looked at the road again, it was alive with possibilities for mayhem. A thin, sour-faced traffic warden caught my eye. He was methodically sticking a ticket to the windscreen of a BMW parked on a double-yellow. I smiled, and moved swiftly in for the strike. As he turned to face me, I promptly poked him in the eye.

I felt, rather than heard, Hill's guffaw inside my skull. The angry warden raised his fist and swung at me. With supernatural speed, I slipped to one side, and the fist connected with a burly, hard-hatted construction worker behind me. He made no noise, but bloody murder flashed in his eyes as he raised his own fists. My skull suddenly rattled from within, as that crazy music roared forth once more.

And the chase had begun!

I felt myself running with astonishing speed, the world whipping into blurs around me as if seen through the window of a rushing train, yet somehow I could still see everything around me, in a full circle. I saw the sequence of pursuers growing the incident by outrage. I saw dresses ripped off, water squirted in faces, bodies skidding on banana peels and painfully hitting the pavement. I heard high-pitched squirrel-like chatterings of shock and outrage from the mob that pursued me, the shattering and tinkling of smashing glass, and that idiot music blasting in my head. And over it all, the chortling of Hill – chortling that sounded oddly triumphant.

As the chase thundered on, I became aware of something. I wasn't feeling amused. I was feeling increasingly exhausted – and increasingly frightened. However hard I ran, the mob saw me, and hurtled at me with violent intent. Seemingly hours later, I found a corner, and a narrow alley just beyond, and ducked into cover. I peeked out carefully as the mob slowed to a bewildered halt. Once more, in less time that it took me to blink sweat from my eyes, clothes returned, bruises vanished from bald heads, all was restored. As my breathing finally returned to normal, I addressed Hill in an angry mutter. "Alright, I've done it now – and it's not what it's cracked up to be. Thanks, but go ride someone else."

Hill's chortle was not comforting. "Sorry, but you're stuck with me. You *asked* me in, and that means that I stay as long as I like."

I realised my error just too late – and what it meant. Hill and I had become a composite entity. Until Hill wanted to go back. And would he *ever* want to? As his laughter echoed in my skull, I suspected the worst.

And the months since then have proved me right. Hill has still not gone: I suspect he never will. He's got me until I die, if I ever do – I worry that Hill's demonic nature has made *me* immortal. The chase goes on throughout my waking hours, but I always escape, somehow, and snatch enough sleep to be ready again the next day. I try staying indoors, but Hill makes us walk outside and it all starts again. And now, he's started showing me things.

Each day, before the chase starts, we walk into a newsagent's. I see ranks of newspapers, their front pages a collage of man-made disasters. Train wrecks, prison riots, ocean liners sinking, red buttons pushed. Headlines shrieking 'Thousands Dead,' 'all hope gone,' 'The End.' Disasters all over the World. Of course, you don't see these editions. Because they don't happen. Because I *stop* them happening. Hill was telling the truth. He was spreading happiness. In the chase, always, there are certain individuals. Individuals whose stress, anger, anxiety are released by the chase. Individuals who thus do *not* go on to fall asleep at the wheels of trains, or draw knives or guns on others, or push ominous red buttons on their desks. Hill doesn't stop *every* disaster in the World – he's only a minor demon – but he stops the more serious ones, in a benign domino theory. It all sounds very lovely. Apart from one thing.

I don't want to do it.

The faces of the people that hare after me are always filled with real fury, genuine hate. If any blows do connect with me, then they *hurt*. And every fresh chase fills me not with exhilaration and joy, but with sick, weary fear. I'm Frankenstein's monster, being chased by an eternal angry mob. As the only time that Hill leaves me is when I sleep, I've taken to fleeing to other countries by night, my wealth (always, maddeningly, one million pounds) easing my flight. But Hill is linked to me, as he said. Sooner or later, the psychic elastic tightens, and he snaps back into me, wherever I am. And it all starts again. A famous author once wondered something along the lines of: 'If you could guarantee the happiness of everyone else in the world, would you sanction the endless torment of just one creature?' For me, that's now become more than just a philosophical bagatelle.

And recognised? Too bloody right I'm *recognised*.

Hill's given me everything that I asked for, and he's even doing good for humanity as a whole. The downbeat ending is purely mine.

Back and forth I go. France, Russia, Canada, Spain, Australia, Greece, America, Turkey... wherever I head, he's not far behind. And neither is the mob.

I'm smoking sixty a day now, and at least one bottle of the local spirits of wherever I am. And I'm never even short of breath. Hill's keeping me healthy. A slow runner is no good at all. The otter is my only comfort, oddly enough. He doesn't just giggle, he speaks fluent English. As we share drinks, he informs me that he isn't really an otter – that he used to be a mongoose called Gef, and could talk even then, and then one day, he made this deal... demons, it seems, are everywhere, for everything.

I've always wanted to see Istanbul, and it seems that I've given Hill the slip for an hour or two, so I order a taxi to the Blue Mosque. The driver is a startlingly beautiful young girl, with a tied-back mane of black hair and a ripe young body doing fascinating things to the front of her vest-top and the seams of her denim shorts (the day is very hot). I'm just relaxing, starting to chat with her, when my hand – *Hill*'s hand – suddenly snakes out and grabs her left breast, squeezing.

"Honk honk", I hear myself say inanely, a leer twisting my face.

She swings to face me, eyes filling with wrath. I notice that she has an uncomfortably muscular arm for such a pretty girl, and know that the blow which strikes me is going to *really* be painful. She swings the cab into the kerb. Her arm folds back, then powers forward. As I slam into the cab door, which pops obligingly open to spill me on the pavement, I hear Hill's mocking mirth. And the first bars of that tune. That *inevitable* tune. The crowd begins to gather, and I know just what is coming next, now and forever, amen.

The girl is standing over me, shouting furiously. The crowd is beginning to react to her anger: I see the need to hunt rising in their eyes. I've noticed that same look in the eyes of everyone who gets caught in the chase, most of all in those of the individuals lucky enough to cause its start. That angry, bewildered stare, that always seems to be asking me the same question.

Who are YOU?

The surrounding crowd gaze at me. The girl has found a baseball bat from somewhere. I heave myself desperately to my feet and start running.

I am Hill.

And who is Hill?

That's easy to answer. It always will be.

*Why, **this** is Hill: nor am I out of it.*

PSILOCYBIN
DAVE SHARROCK

I have always been fascinated by a series of memories that do not belong to me, nor should belong to any sane man. This leads me, through the linear process of applied logic, to conclude that I am no longer a sane man. For when I recount details and specifics to friends, colleagues or those who purport scholarly expertise in the intricacies of the human mind, the response has been universally one of revulsion. Revulsion of spirit, I should add. Not the kind of repugnance associated with the presence of some fetid feature of rot and decay or the noisome odour of drains in dire need of clearing. Their reaction is a metaphysical flinch from that which the mortal brain does not and will not comprehend.

The situation developed in my early 20s during a period of belated post-teenage exuberance and experimentation with intoxicants. What began as simple fumblings among friends with ethanol and amphetamines soon escalated to encompass more potent fungoid excesses. Morphine diacetate, injected intravenously, morphine and similar opiates and then Psilocybin mushrooms. This latter triggered the awakening of those memories which, in turn, unnerved, terrified then gradually fascinated me.

The memories emerged at first as dark dreams, sweeping but simple dioramas where I, as some bird of other-worldly origin, would soar over endless vistas of geodesic lattice-work scattered with cyclopean architecture, tumbled mega-cities of obsidian and granite blocks against a white-spattered backdrop of stars, galaxies and expanding gas forms, amorphous dying stars and nebulae. I would wake from these phantasmagorical flights drenched in sweat and breathing hard, craving light so that my fingers would fumble for the nearest switch.

As the dreams continued, night after night, it seemed to me that the imagery gained dimension. The landscapes, shallow and surreal in previous visits, became firm and detailed. I would swoop low across meadows of strange luminous grey grass, wheel through eye-shaped hollows in Brobdingnagian stone formations and rise to ascend the faces of gargantuan black cliffs. I was a winged Gulliver exploring the land of giants and so lucid and alluring were the dreams of this time that even though I awoke with a sinking dread clawing at the walls of my soul, there was also present a crushing disappointment. I feared that I had returned to the mundanity of the everyday for once and all. A horror unequalled and incomparable to any emotion I had thus far experienced worried at my every thought.

That I might close my eyes and dream only of the prosaic and routine impressions of terrestrial life and never more inhabit that Kafkaesque wonderland of my dreams; that I might be tethered forever to the Earth and the sack-like mass of my own flightless body, such fears wrought within me an angst I would spare even the foulest and lowest of human life.

But my fears were unnecessary. The dreams did not abate but instead intensified further and morphed in strange quasi-perceptual ways so that the threshold between the memory of the dream and the memory of waking events was smeared and I could no longer discern between recollection of the real and recollection of the surreal.

I would prepare to bed, many hours from waking after a night of mystical dreaming, only to feel that mere minutes before I had been cruising in unknown heights above that matrix mesh of intertwined dimensional landscapes, flying between glistening fangs of fused stone or windowless basalt towers, buttressed by angles of cosmic design. Friends and family would inform me of my trance-like condition during these phases and spoke of their fears for the stability of my mind. But I cared not. A point was fast approaching where the ties of mundane life were growing wearisome compared with the free spirited flight of my alter-ego; the Escher bird of outlandish skies, boundless in a quest to explore and only to explore.

The dreams, the memories, the desire to cross forever into that nether realm so removed from all that humanity holds dear, culminated in one final memory. A landing of the bird on strange feet and strange legs whose rubbery countenance I could feel as surely as I feel my own human limbs. I landed upon the steps of a prodigious temple, formed of many multi-layered slabs of colossal size, and climbed to the pinnacle. There I encountered an open shrine of equally numbing enormity, lined with columns so immense that each was a tower fashioned with doors and scribed about their girth with cuneiform text and pictographs I shudder now to recall.

At the heart of the shrine stood a thing whose image is embedded in my mind as after burn hovers upon the retina after the flash of some painful light. A fungoid growth, vast as a skyscraper, capped with a bulbous, pulsating helmet of such enormity that, to begin with, my human senses mistook the thing for the roof of the shrine. Ribbed it was and alive. Vibrant with thoughts that pulsed like shockwaves from the heart of the mighty trunk and filled the air with the noxious stench of algae and mould.

I bowed on stork-like legs and spread my wings. The fungoid acknowledged my presence and congratulated me on securing the soul of another of Earth's dreamers. It was then that my mind and the thinking machination of my flying host merged and I could access truths of such frightening magnitude that I fear my sanity snapped and I became like a spectator in a crowd. I marvelled and wondered as the fungoid spoke of envoys flung from galactic profundities so distant and strange that man should travel the stars forever and yet stumble upon even the fringe of mushroom domains. Spores as craft, spreading the hive mind consciousness of the horror beyond eternity, embedding themselves in the roots and soil of alien worlds to grow as that Terrene flora so commonly known to the peoples of the Earth as the poppy and the Psilocybin mushroom.

A gulf of essence and distance spans the chasm between the lifeforms of Earth and the creatures of my dream memories, and yet we are ever connected. For in the shadow of the great fungoid I shook with terror, even as an angel enthralled to my daemon master. For here was evil unmitigated, unfiltered and abroad. No master of the universe stands between us and them, only the choices men make and the weakness of the soul.

HIAB_X
DAVID J RODGER

Matthias Nathan Plunkett appeared on the pale shore like a man stepping out of thin air. A headless body of dark clay covered in an ash blue dust; the decapitated figure carried a bronze box in strong, long-fingered hands. The severed stump of the broad neck was smooth and bloodless, the clay neatly flattened down to conceal any internal workings of his mysterious form.

The box gleamed in the furnace-red glare of the setting Star, five of its sides etched in symbols that were half as old as the distant planet Mars. The sixth side was made of a transparent crystal that revealed the contents inside: a pink, fleshy and bearded face of the man-child, now aged through forty-three years, eyes bulging wide and swivelling as they tracked the creeping, crawling progress of the clockwork demons that scuttled around inside.

His mouth was open, lips twisting, tongue quivering, as it exhaled a torrent of tormented words that remained sealed inside the box along with the head.

In the moment after his appearance the black waters behind him rippled for a moment as a trans-dimensional breeze gusted outwards and died.

Despite the isolated head's terror, the body remained calm and began to walk along the shoreline; heavy feet sinking into gelatinous grains of sand – each footfall leaving a gently glowing impression. The body seemed to understand whilst the bronze box soundlessly babbled.

Where was this place? And why was the Dreamer so far from his realm?

Fragments of memory began to rain down upon the beach. Chunks the size of houses and lumps no bigger than a fist; broken masonry, the outlines of familiar places and shattered figures of friends and family from the past. The present. The future. The body continued walking, building a steady unrelenting stride, purpose now in the golem muscles of clay legs.

Inside the box a clockwork demon paused over one eye and plucked at fold of sweat-speckled skin that was the eyelid, with metal pincer claws. The eye bulged wider, the jaw cracked open in utter shock. The demon inspected the curving lens and began to probe the elastic surface with a single razor-pointed barb.

But immediately withdrew as a reflection slid across the glassy outer film: a shape like a beetle, but much larger; sleek lines that were all bright fluorescent light. The body had remembered what the head had not. And brought it back to this place. On the edges of the celestial rim where the dead and dying mix breath with those who still live.

A bad fever. A touch of the Dark Horseman's bone claw on his left cheek.

Inside the box the head stopped screaming and stared at the Scarab Beetle ship, which stood awaiting the Dreamer's return. A squat, recurved hull covered in ethereal combat paint, the colours impossible to describe in the red glare of the Star. Broad lips twitched with a recalled smile; the head realised it was his ship and this was his way back home.

THE LOST BROTHER

SIMON BRAKE

I don't know what I expected to see in the mirror. Sadness, I suppose, regret and heartache etched into my features. But what strikes me most is how tired I look. My eyes lack their usual alert focus, the eyelids heavy. In the dim light of the flickering candle the smudges of dirt and blood on my face hide amongst the shadows, but they're there, if you know where to look. I look like a beaten old man, older than my years. There's something that keeps me staring in the mirror, holding my own gaze, as if this is a brief respite from doing what I need to do. In these few fleeting seconds I see my own face, familiar and solid amongst all this chaos. I tell myself that the worst of it is over. And maybe I believe that, for a second.

I look back down into the sink, my hands under the running water. As it cascades off my hands and swirls into the plughole I can see it is almost running clear now. The sleeves of my shirt are still splattered with dried blood, as dark as ink in this half-light. I find myself thinking of the bottle of black ink my uncle has sitting on his writing desk, impenetrable darkness locked within glass. Waiting to be opened, to be spilled out across a page in my uncle's scrawl. Or perhaps my own.

I realise I must make an account of these past days and nights. Of my connection to this place, and these people. One last glance at the man in the mirror with the tired eyes, and I retire to the study, to my uncle's desk. The bottle of ink waits there, patiently, as I check the drawers for paper. Finding some, I settle myself into the large leather chair and compose myself. Looking up I see, once more, my reflection, the candle light painting it in the window over the top of the night sky beyond.

Here then, is my story, should I not live to see the dawning of another day.

***

My name is Matthew.

I knew these woods and the nearby town of Hepworth as a child, but until I returned here some months ago I'd not been for close to thirteen years. These woods are dark and ominous, and not at all how I remember them, long ago, before I knew what lurked in the shadows. Thirteen years. Half my life, give or take a few months. I was thirteen when the world ended, when the sky turned a sickly toxic yellow with the rising sun, when robots started turning on their creators, when viruses spread across the globe and wiped out swathes of people. The end of the world.

Of course, it didn't end. Not for everyone, at least.

I'm part of a lost generation, I figure. There's the generation that came before us, had lived many years by the time they witnessed what seemed to be the world's end. Seen before on so many screens in countless disaster movies, or prophesised in numerous religious texts and conspiracy theories, when the end came people panicked, desperately trying to hold things together as bodies piled up in the streets, bloodied, disease-ridden, abuzz with flies. These were our parents, our teachers, our leaders. Our role models. These are the ones who saw their perfect worlds crumble.

Conversely there's the generations that came after us, those who have been born in the years since the world ended, a generation that has never known anything but this post-apocalyptic landscape, has never known a world which wasn't inhabited by terrifying 'orcs' or 'zombies', and has therefore been better equipped to adapt to it, better taught how to deal with the here and now.

And then there's us. The true children of the apocalypse. Youngsters who were just discovering what life had to offer, the future constantly unfolding and showing us glimpses of new wonders just inches from our finger tips, only to have it all torn to shreds in front of us, our hopes and dreams dashed, our educations snatched away and rendered, in many cases, meaningless. I lost family and friends during the chaos that erupted across the globe, but many of the other children who buckled under that same sense of loss became friends and family in their stead. Surviving the initial disasters that befell humanity was one thing, but often that was a case of instinct, of following the biological imperative to keep alive, to keep swimming to the surface, to keep drawing breath. It was in the quiet periods that followed, heart wrenching moments in the late hours of the night where we considered everything that ever mattered being lost, not knowing if we could face another day - those were the trying times. For those of us struggling with our own sense of identity and emotional fragility, as young people do regardless of background interference, it was a baptism by fire. And, in many ways, those scars are still healing.

Dad died this year, in a small town on the French coast, called Ambleteuse. My mother died when I was young, and my sister Jessie died within weeks of the first virus striking, as we fled from the Hepworth. The journey back was prompted, in part, by wanting to see if anything remained of the place we once called home, to revisit memories of happier times. But the main reason I decided to dig up the past was in the hope that our extended family also survived the end of the world.

Dad had always been close to his brother since Mum died and we, in turn, came to see our cousins regularly. I still clearly remember the last time we saw them all, Peter, Andrew, Uncle Jack and Aunt Lara. They'd come over in the wake of the news, shortly following the Yellow Dawn incident, the adults chatting in the kitchen whilst we kids played. The media networks at that time had become unreliable, coverage spotty, reports alternating between deliver news of catastrophic events and experts trying to downplay the seriousness of those events. As kids we didn't really grasp what was happening, but I could tell that there was much our parents were concerned about. As day gave way to night, and my younger sister and cousins were tucked up in bed, my curiosity got the better of me and I listened in on a conversation between our father and uncle. It turned out to be the last time the two brothers saw each other.

Uncle Jack and Aunt Lara were begging Dad to bring our family to stay with them, in their house out in the woods. It would be safe, they said, secluded, well away from urban centres where malfunctioning robots might lurk, or the teeming throngs of people in which deadly viruses might hide. But Dad had decided on a plan of his own, to take Jessie and I towards the English Channel, to get a boat to Europe. London, ever hopeful that science would pull humanity through. The following morning our two families went our separate ways, our uncle taking his off into the woods some way north of Hepworth, our father taking us and the bare minimum we could carry on a journey south.

Needless to say, on reflection, our uncle made the better choice. Neither family remained unscathed, but those who fled to the woods at least had some semblance of normally, of stability. Those of us who optimistically set off looking for a better future found nothing but disappointment.

The further south we travelled, the more chaos we saw. People desperately fled from those places where the virus was said to have appeared, or tried to find their way home to loved ones, crowds of people piling onto trains and buses, occasional accidents where travellers fell in front of vehicles under the weight of people pushing from behind. We avoided the cities, even as we headed towards London, until it became clear that the capital was faring no better than those cities we'd avoided. We met people heading north; trying to escape from London, thinking safety lay that way, it quickly becoming clear that nowhere was safe. As we tried to bypass the capital we were joined by others fleeing from it, a familiar look of desperation and panic in their eyes.

Beyond London, heading south into Surrey, we found less people travelling against us, back towards London, as if everyone knew it had fallen, that the only safety lay in fleeing across the sea now. To some it was like an exodus, people leaving the only homes they'd ever known to find some sort of promised land, somewhere safe, somewhere untouched by disaster. As we passed Woking our father, always one to value literature over religion, was compelled to compare it more with the events from of the War of the World, recalling passages of how Londoners fled from the Martians in their droves. To our childish imaginations we could only wonder at what the truth was. What if the arrival of the Martians was heralded not with a green flare in space but with a yellow haze? What if this time bacteria were the ally of the invaders, and the enemy of mankind?

Our nights were plagued by nightmares, often fed by the stories we heard in daylight, speculation about what was at the root of the world's end. Aliens, some said. God's judgement, said others. A viral outbreak on an unprecedented scale sending everyone crazy, suggested a third group. Dad wasn't too sure himself, despite his literary asides ('The chances of anything coming from Mars, are a million to one,' he clarified). None of us knew what to make of the various tales we heard, and the further we travelled, the more we heard. One guy had witnessed a robot massacre, had run for cover, ushered by armed police, as if he were escaping a terrorist attack. Several people told us that the dead were rising, struck down by the virus and then clambering to their feet once more, the flesh festering and falling from their bones. Others had heard more, or perhaps witnessed one of these individuals, claiming they were not the people they were when they'd died, having instead animated as the hosts of demonic creatures that warped them into hideous countenance. Safe to say that none of us slept soundly those first few weeks.

We weren't far south of Woking when it became clear that Jessie was in a worse state than the rest of us. After she began coughing, we tried to keep away from other people. Dad was distraught, understandably, and wouldn't leave her side for several nights. I can only think that he must have blamed himself. I did too, for a long time after, although I never stopped loving him. He always thought he was doing what was best for us. Jessie looked so peaceful when she finally passed, as if sleeping. In many ways I'm glad that she was taken quickly, and remained forever beautiful and pure in our eyes, rather than survive and become something monstrous. I think Dad's mind might have broken completely, had she 'Changed'. I still feel guilty about thinking like that though. Does being thankful my sister died make me a bad person?

I can't remember the official estimate for the death toll, but it was somewhere above seventy percent of the population. Uncle Jack had been right. The cities saw most of those deaths. Outside the cities the odds were more skewed in our favour. But the deaths that hit us hit us hard, people taken one at a time. When Jessie fell ill we did what we could to ensure we didn't fall ill ourselves, but I don't know whether our success lay with our precautions, a genetic fluke, or just plain luck.

Jessie's final resting place was atop a hill, buried near the edge of the woods that covered it. Dad had wrapped up her body in a blanket, then laid it in a shallow grave. As he began to fill in the hole, the soil scattering across the white linen, I turned away, unable to watch. We said our goodbyes to her as we looked out across an English countryside that, for a long while, felt peaceful. At this distance we couldn't see anyone, couldn't hear anything bar the sound of birds nearby. We remained to watch the sun sink behind the horizon, dusk still slightly discoloured like a bruise, to see the stars come out, one by one. For a long time we said nothing, just waited. Cried a little. Huddled together. Our first night without Jessie.

The world's a very different place now, of course. That was half a lifetime ago, but I still remember that night fondly. Even now, when I'm out in the wilderness or gazing out across the rooftops of a dead city, I'll find myself gazing skywards at the stars, picking out constellations and thinking of Jessie. Imagining, perhaps, that she's gazing down.

Are you up there now, sister? I've found myself wondering that a lot recently.

My father and I pressed on and made it to the coast. Convinced life would be better on the other side we tried to get across the English Channel in a boat with several other desperate families, scared parents and children huddled together. We looked towards the horizon, towards safety and hope for the future. When we reached French shores we found much the same chaos as we'd seen in Britain. Refugees had fled from around the continent to the northern coastline, hoping that crossing lay across the Channel. News reports clarified that events were unfolding much the same the whole globe over. And so we gave up trying to flee, realising there was nowhere to flee to anymore.

We supported each other, Dad and I, strangers in a strange land, as so many people were back then. Once governments - or what was left of them - began to take control of the situation some sense of normality began to creep in. But with the dead outnumbering the living, it was never going to be easy. The two of us, and some of those we'd crossed the Channel with, eventually settled in a shanty town somewhere west of Calais. Me, well, I adapted, as most kids did. Dad, however, had been broken by our experiences. I stayed with him into my early twenties, looking after him, ensuring we had food and shelter, but ultimately we were safe. I finally resolved to travel, to see what I could of this new world, confident that Dad would be okay. And he was, for a while. But maybe I should've spent a bit more time with Dad over these last few years.

My father died a month ago. It took me some time to arrange passage by boat back to Britain, but I finally made it, earning my passage through manual labour. Britain has changed somewhat from the place I knew, but then I expected that. Cities now husks of their former selves, abandoned towers that serve as a warning.

Other communities have thrived, to replace those cities of old, wielding modern technology. Small communities have sprung up in rural areas away from the cities, attempting to distance themselves from the horrors of the cities, of virus and technology, defending themselves against the few bandits and orcs the countryside has to offer. The journey across England, retracing the route I took with my father and sister, led me into few encounters with such threats, and in fact gave me the opportunity to sample hospitality in some of those small communities that have formed since the world ended. Once it was clear I wasn't a monster or troublemaker I was welcomed in with requests of news about the world beyond. Many of these people will never leave their home towns. They're too scared about what lurks out there in the shadows; their imaginations fired up about the hungry dead, about debase orcs, about killer robots.

The truth be told I've never worried too much about the monsters. Zombies rarely wander far from the cities, so most of your encounters with them are going to be ones you're at least prepared for. I've never seen a killer robot myself. And I've never had trouble with orcs. They're feral, sure, and desperation sometimes turns them dangerous, but they're mostly trying to carve out their own niche in the remains of this world. No, it's always been organised groups of humans that have caused me the greatest trouble. Desperation is one thing, but greed is quite another. Greed and fear.

When I finally reached Hepworth two weeks ago, it became clear that much had changed, aside from the way the trees and bushes had begun to intrude on the town. It didn't take long to discover one of the grisly totems that had been nailed up along the route into town, a warning to those who ventured down this road. A warning, it became clear from the succession of similar corpses, specifically for orcs. Decapitated disfigured heads peered down from sticks, unblinking black eyes staring out of faces that looked beaten, bloodied and bruised. It was impossible to discern whether the appearance was the result of the virus that corrupted their flesh many years ago, or more recent violence at the hands of their killers. In any case, this had not been the welcome home I had been looking forward to.

The town had been left to fall apart, dirt and plant life competing to take over the remnants of the houses. As I walked through the crumbling streets I observed that people still lived here but few looked as if they were the original inhabitants. Eyes watched me suspiciously as I followed familiar streets back towards the house I had once called home. I barely recognised it.

As I picked through the remains, much of the furniture damaged by water and neglect, an old man, one who had lived in Hepworth back when I was a child, found me and offered me some food and shelter, and a few answers. He told me how the town was now little more than a refuge for people passing through, or those who'd been unable to get away since the time death walked the streets and lay waste to so many. A few families still struggled to make a living from the land, but largely the town had become home to those willing to earn their bed and board through killing the savage monsters that lurked in the woods. The orcs. I nodded my understanding, but it saddened me. Not only because I knew orcs to be more than simply monsters, but also because of Hepworth's old town history.

As a child I'd heard the story of the Great Plague that had ravaged Europe. It spread across England, but got no further north than Hepworth. After the townsfolk decided to keep the infected and the healthy apart, each in a separate half of the town, thirteen people died, a significant number when Hepworth was still a small village. Their deaths were commemorated with the planting of thirteen trees and the annual Hepworth Feast, every June. Approximately five centuries on and it seemed the victims of this more recent plague had not been treated with as much respect. Instead they had been hunted down and slaughtered, their remains left out to fester under an uncaring sun, pecked at by carrion birds. I wondered if, by some cruel twist of fate, any of these unfortunate souls had ended up hanging from the branches of one of those thirteen trees planted to mark the end of the Great Plague.

I told the old man a little of my own story, of my family, of how my father had hoped to find safety in the cities, whilst my uncle had opted to retreat into the woods. Of how upon the death of my father I had returned, to see if anyone else had survived. And the old man nodded, and told me they had. That one of my cousins, Peter, came into town every month or so, to trade food or information. His brother Andrew, the old man added, had died long ago, a victim of the first virus. Their parents had, as many people had, struggled to live beyond the death of their loved ones, my aunt dying some few winters after the end of the world. The last the old man had heard, from Peter himself, was that Uncle Jack was still alive, albeit in failing health.

I asked how Peter was, the last time he'd seen him, and the old man went quiet. When he finally spoke, he looked me in the eye and related, in hushed tones, how Peter was always stoic, but that last time he'd been in town he'd been even graver than usual. Because that last time he'd brought someone with him. A young man, only recently arrived in town, but barely recognisable, eye sockets bloody and sightless, cheeks covered in trails of dried and flaking gore. He clutched a blanket to himself, with bandaged hands that lacked digits, and when he could be convinced to part with it the state of his body beneath was made evident, also partially bandaged but seeping with blood and puss. Malnourished too.

I'm sure it took me a moment to find my voice, but I asked the old man what had happened. He explained, grimly, that this was some poor soul who'd fallen afoul of the Tattergaunt and had survived to tell the tale. Or perhaps might have told the tale, had he not been driven to the edge of sanity by his experience. The Tattergaunt, he explained, was a monster that haunted the forests, worse than any zombie or orc, which terrorised any unfortunate that wandered into its territory at night. A bogeyman that lurked in the shadows between the trees and wore the skins of its victims. It had never ventured as far as the town, but there had been those who had decided to take on the challenge to kill the Tattergaunt, and who had never returned.

Peter found this most recent victim bound to a tree. He imagined he'd been there for several days without food or drink, and tortured for much of that time. He could barely speak. For a moment Peter had wondered if the man was also lacking a tongue, but after accepting water thirstily he sputtered a thank you and begged to be taken away before the creature returned. He was exhausted and terrified, having spent many hours screaming in the dark. He said little more on the journey into town, Peter had said. There didn't seem to be much of his mind left.

I asked the old man what Peter had done next, after he'd brought the man back to town and he told me he'd picked up some supplies, food mostly, and then headed back into the woods. Some of the townsfolk had implored that he not head back, not with the Tattergaunt roaming the area, but he was adamant. His father was alone at the house, and could not deal without him. Eventually, reluctantly, they ceased their protests. He'd lived in the woods all these years, and had never run afoul of the orcs or the Tattergaunt before. And, sure, some people thought him slightly crazy, living in the woods rather than in the safety of the town, but Peter was a large and somewhat imposing man nowadays, and if anyone could take care of himself it was probably him.

That had been maybe three weeks before my return to Hepworth.

My initial instinct was to set off to find my cousin before darkness fell, against the old man's advice. The Tattergaunt, he warned me, will do for you as it did for the last fellow. Best not to risk the woods, better to wait in town until Peter returned again in a week or so. At the very least, the old man cautioned, wait until morning.

Some of the town's newer inhabitants echoed the old man's sentiments. Though no-one could tell me what exactly the creature was, several of the men claimed to have seen it. Tall and spidery, said one, although with four limbs like a man. Two glowing orbs in the shadows, said another, and a mouthful of pointed white teeth. It's one of those machines, suggested a third, something dark and alien and mechanical that's left the city to stalk the wilderness. The only person in town I figured might know for sure wasn't saying anything to anyone, bandaged and sedated and terrified of any unexpected noise.

I didn't linger in town longer than necessary, didn't try to get any more answers. The only answer I needed was to the question of whether my cousin and uncle were still alive.

The road heading north out of Hepworth was lined by the same grim trophies as I'd found approaching the town from the south. The faces, at least, were turned away from me as I approached them, looking out towards the trees. I kept my eyes on the road ahead. I felt dead eyes on my back as I walked on but wondered, dreaded, what might be in the woods looking back.

The road itself was familiar, twists and turns dimly recalled from childhood, but the canopy of trees seemed more expansive than those memories suggested. I could barely see the sky above but there was enough light filtering through the leaves to infuse the shadows with colour and shape. The people in town told me that the woods had, for a long time, been 'orc territory', but with the stories of the terrifying Tattergaunt it was doubtful even those monsters were safe. I pulled my coat closer around me, shuddering at the thought of the creature, and pressed on.

I stuck to the road, of course. Childhood stories always reminded kids not to stray from the path but common sense demanded it here. If I had left the road I might have headed in the wrong direction altogether, with no familiar landmarks to guide me. If I had chosen to walk where the trees huddled closer together I'd have sacrificed the half-light of the main shadow for the darker shade where something might've been lying in wait. I proceeded slowly, checking behind me as I went, pausing at the distant chattering of a bird softly, alert to the slightest noise. Had I made a mistake but setting out on my own? What if something found me before I found my uncle's house? What if Peter, having found one victim of the Tattergaunt and rescued him, had been claimed by the monster himself upon his journey back? I peered into the darkness with increasing alarm, wondering if I'd see anyone else, dead or alive, tied to the trunk of a tree. Heading into the great unknown suddenly felt like the sort of impulsive act my dad would've done. I instinctively glanced upwards, towards stars I knew I couldn't see even if it were night time. Maybe my father watches down from heaven now, I wondered. Or maybe he can't see me at all.

It took me a few hours to reach the turn off for my uncle's house. There'd been no traffic heading in either direction, not that I expected any. The debris of broken branches and leaves suggested very little came through to disturb this route. The side road, however, had almost entirely been claimed by the woods, the branches overhead threatening to tangle together, to block out all light. There were a few breaks in the cover ahead, stabs of daylight through the thick branches above, but for the most part the dirt road resembled a tunnel into darkness. Here I began, once more, to doubt the wisdom of my journey alone. But, knowing that this was a journey my cousin must've made many times before, I ducked my head down and pressed on.

This smaller road, again somewhat familiar and yet different to how I remembered it, seemed quieter than the main road out of town. Although I still saw birds amongst the branches they were quick to dart away, their bird song now more irregular and distant. The restless tree branches shifted with the wind, leaves whispering closer than they had before, only occasionally admitting glimpses of the blue sky above. But I knew there was not much further to go now and resolved to pick up some speed.

And then something moved, just out of sight to my right.

I froze. Slowly, without any sudden movements, I slid my right hand into my jacket, towards where I kept my small automatic holstered. I'm not sure what it was I saw, but it was large, something the height of a man. Perhaps taller. A smudge of shadow out of the corner of my eye, a blur of movement. It was hard to tell, a vague dark shape blended in with the darkness all around it. Certainly there was no tell-tale sign of sunlight glinting off polished metal, or reflecting from eyes turned my way. Just enough ambient light to give the impression of something that wasn't just a spooked animal running for cover. And so I began to run.

The trail ahead gave no indication of how close to the end I was, the frequent bends giving me hope that I was almost there then snatching it away with the reveal of a further turning ahead. I was surrounded by bushes that tugged at my clothes as I ran, branches that snagged at my hair, my mind not entirely convinced it was just the plants either side of me. I ducked down, arms shielding my face, trying to keep low as I proceed, trying to listen out for anything but only hearing my own stumbling footsteps.

And then I saw something, something darting across the trail ahead, right to left, some distance ahead in the gloom. Something, or someone. For a few seconds a figure, barely visible against the trees beyond it, looked my way, before slipping away from the road once more. Human perhaps. Possibly an orc. Or could it have been something else, something more monstrous? It didn't look like the tall thin creature I've been expecting. And yet my mind raced, my heart pounded. This could be the creature that pulls out eyes and bites off fingers. I panicked, half expecting arms to reach out from between the trees, or to turn and see a barely human shape looming over me.

And I turned, slowly, expecting the worst.

There was nothing there.

I turned back.

The same trail stretched ahead, into darkness.

I did not move, could not move, for maybe a minute, my ears straining to hear even the slightest noise. My breathing came in shallow, quiet gasps. Nothing. Another minute. I crouched, fingers stretching downwards until I had my hand pressed to the ground, not knowing if I dared to move, or if the creature was watching me. I couldn't see anything either side of me, just the trail and the trees ahead of me, and more darkness beyond.

And then, not knowing how far I still had to go, I broke into a sprint, repeating the mantra: I don't want to die here.

I crashed through the bushes, a branch catching me in the face as I did, a stinging pain that registered but could not stop me. I was no longer quiet, no longer aware of any noise except that which I was now making. Pushing forward on uneven ground into the dark, adrenalin pumping, each step feeling like it might be my last before I lost my balance and fell onto my face. But I didn't fall, didn't stumble. I kept running until I glimpsed hope. A break in the trees ahead.

I thought of Jessie then, imagined her willing me on, finding my way to safety, and I laughed. For a moment the idea that reaching the end of the road would keep me safe from anything that might be pursuing me struck me as ridiculous, but then my hope became somewhat more concrete, as I saw the canopy of branches give way to a clearing, and within the clearing the looming shape of my uncle's house. Running towards the front door, never pausing to look over my shoulder, my foot caught on something half buried in the garden. Somehow I kept my balance, but was almost on all fours as I scrambled up the steps, to the door, calling out Peter's name. I banged my fists on the door, desperately pleading to be let in, refusing to turn to face whatever might be pursuing me. And then the door opened, and I threw myself forward, into the arms of the young man I recognised as my cousin.

***

I passed out from exhaustion, as far as I could tell, and didn't awaken til early that evening. It was strange, awakening in a room from my childhood, particularly after finding my own childhood home in ruins. Peter found me at the window staring out towards the road leading into the clearing, where I imagined the Tattergaunt had been at my heels. He told me later that he watched me standing there for a good few minutes before he knocked on the doorframe and asked me to join him and his father downstairs for something to eat. I hugged him, and he hugged back, but he felt distant even as he smiled and told me how good it was to see me.

It wasn't easy to get the conversation flowing, not at first. I mean, you know, it's been thirteen years. And thirteen of the most terrifying years. We were both children when the world ended, and here we sat, two grown men, strangers in so many ways. Linked by blood, by family, but moulded into two very distinct people by our separate experiences. And Uncle Jack wasn't the same person he'd been. His experiences had been too much for him, having lost his youngest son, his wife, and finally his mind. But, slowly, we told our tales of the events that had shaped us, and became friends anew. This is often the case for us, those of the lost generation, but it was so great to be finding friendship with real family that were, for so long, lost to me.

The first thing we spoke of was the Tattergaunt, the creature that stalked the woods by night. Peter's reaction was a mixture of conflicting emotions; he was glad to see me but was close to anger regarding the manner of my arrival, choking back tears at the idea that I might have made it so close to home only to die in the woods, yards from the house. He said he'd never seen the creature himself, only heard the stories. But he'd seen the bodies. Animal carcasses, mostly, but increasingly human hunters that had come this deep into the forest. He'd heard things too. Whispering noises, he said. He wondered perhaps if it was some sort of wronged spirit. I don't believe in ghosts and told him as much, and he smiled. "Neither did I, once. But once you know the dead can rise you start to wonder what other impossible things might be possible."

I asked him why he didn't move back to town with his father, to find safety in numbers. He looked sad as he gazed around the house, before finally saying "This is all I have left now. I don't know if I could give up all the memories this place holds." He picked a picture up from a nearby shelf, an old photo that showed our two fathers together, their wives, their children. All of us, so long ago, oblivious to what the future had in store. Happy.

We talked of lost loved ones. Peter showed me the small grave markers in the garden, dedicated to his mother and brother, and I realised what I must have stumbled over as I ran for the front door, convinced I was about to die. Peter sadly told me of their fates. Andrew, he said, had succumbed to a virus maybe a month after they'd left town. Isolation has postponed its touch only so long, and when it finally came for them it claimed only Peter's younger brother. He didn't survive, didn't become one of The Changed. He died horribly, by Peter's account, convulsing, blood bubbling on his lips, eyes bulging from his head. As Peter relived his last moments with his lost brother, he looked drained. I put my arm around him, considering how much luckier I had been with my sister.

Andrew's death changed everything. Peter lost his best friend - and his parents lost a child - in a most hideous way. They buried him in the garden. Their mother took his death particularly badly, as news spread of other events around the world. She became convinced that the dead would rise again, that she would wake one night and find that Andrew had clawed his way out of his grave and would be sitting at the end of her bed. As months became years she was more and more convinced that the nightmares she had were real.

One morning Aunt Lara never woke up. Perhaps it was a heart attack. Or a stroke. They never had a doctor come to confirm the diagnosis. They just buried her, alongside her son, hoping that she could rest more peacefully than she did in those last years of her life.

I related my own accounts, of course. I told my cousin and my uncle about our journey. About how Jessie fell ill and died suddenly, and now rested under the trees on a hill near London. Peter listened intently, a tear trickling down one cheek as I spoke of my sister. I rubbed my eyes, pausing a moment before then explaining how my father had been up until the time when he died. My uncle hugged me and I found myself unable to continue. It was a sad hug, full of regret. As much as I wish I could see Dad one last time, I know my uncle wished he could've said goodbye to his brother.

As keenly as I feel the loss of my sister, I felt bad for both my uncle and cousin for losing their brothers. Peter especially, as he and Andrew had done everything together, even if Andrew had been a pain in the arse. Peter had set aside a room in the attic, he told me, where he kept his brother's things. He clearly still missed his brother as I'd often wake up in the night to hear him pottering around up there. He asked me not to go up there myself, that there are things up there that he and his father would rather not have disturbed. But I'll admit, I was curious about what he kept there to occupy him.

I'm still curious as to what is up there.

Coming back here, seeing my cousin and uncle again, was like coming home. On that first night, gazing up at the stars, I could imagine that my whole family were here, those that had passed on and those who were left behind. For a moment I had something precious.

I should've known better than to expect that to last.

I'm not sure how long I suspected the truth. Maybe as far back as that first night, when my cousin spoke about the death of his brother and the suffering of his mother. But certainly, after that first night, as Peter showed me how the house was supplied with power from a windmill he'd had some help building many years ago, how they grew their own food out back, and how they honestly had never had any trouble with the local orc population or the savage Tattergaunt I began to get more and suspicious. Suspecting that, perhaps, I wasn't being told the entire truth. I guess it wasn't just the secret room either. Peter would often still be up when I retired for the evening, and wouldn't get up for a good few hours after I'd been awake each morning.

This evening I discovered why.

Not through my own prying, I should add, but through the arrival of unexpected guests at the house this evening. There was a knock on the door. Peter looked at me, a flash of concern across his face. "We don't get visitors," he said, slowly getting out of his chair. "Not before you turned up," remarked Uncle Jack, smiling. The knock came a second time, no less urgent than the first, and Peter crossed the room to answer it. I couldn't see who it was from where I was sitting, but my cousin turned to me and said "Friends of yours." called Peter.

It was the old man.

He seemed relieved to see my face when I joined them at the door. "I was worried," he said, "You took off into the woods and I never saw you again, so I figured I'd come out here and check things were okay. Make sure you got here in one piece and not lots of little ones." His companions laughed, and I looked at them for the first time. A fat white man in biker's leathers with a shaven head stood at the bottom of the steps, slightly ahead of a black guy with multi-coloured dreadlocks and an old army issue trench coat. They both carried rifles. I noticed, for the first time, that the old man had a shotgun resting at his side.

Peter invited the three of them in, offering them a chance to take the weight off of their feet and have something to eat and drink before they headed back. They didn't stay too long, but I had the impression they were making my cousin feel uncomfortable. The old man was pleasant enough, at first, but after a while he wondered aloud why the three of us were living out in the woods, out in orc country. Peter simply told him that he didn't have a problem with orcs. They left them to themselves, as long as they didn't bother the orcs. "What about the Tattergaunt?" asked the old man. After a pause Peter shook his head. "It only comes out at night, doesn't it? You'd have to be mad to go out into the woods at night."

The old man nodded his agreement. "Sure," he said, "that'd be crazy." A look passed between his two companions. "We'll need to be going before the sun gets much lower in the sky," he added, "or who knows what trouble we might run into."

They didn't stay much longer. Uncle Jack absent-mindedly waved goodbye to them as they left. "Four," he muttered, waggling the four fingers of one hand as he did so.

I spent a little time that afternoon talking to my uncle about his childhood, about my father, about the good old days before the world fell apart. Uncle Jack had good days, I suppose, but those were mostly the days when his mind did him the courtesy of forgetting what had happened over the last thirteen years. Peter had something on his mind and excused himself, saying he needed to get something from town, that he'd have to hurry before it got too dark. I asked if he wanted me to accompany him but asked that I stay behind to keep his father company. I was happy to do so, but at the same time couldn't help but worry about my cousin. Regardless of what he thought about the orcs I couldn't help but think about the poor man he'd rescued, and of the chance that he might fall foul of the Tattergaunt.

As the afternoon stretched towards evening, and we lit candles to illuminate the room, the conversation with my uncle drifted from memories of his childhood to memories of my own, the childhood I shared with my sister and my cousins. I found myself thinking, as I had several times, of the room upstairs where Andrew's belongings had been stored and once my uncle had started to doze decided that there was no better time to satisfy my curiosity. Having ascended the stairs to the attic landing, I discovered the door I remembered from childhood. Since the house was supposed to be empty apart from my uncle and me, I was surprised to see light dancing from beneath the door, from what I could only assume was candlelight. Confused, worried even, that Peter had left a lit candle in the room before leaving several hours ago, I approached the door quickly, and tried to open it. The door remained closed, locked.

There was movement on the other side of the door.

Then silence.

Then a voice, low and inhuman. "Peter?"

I jumped back. There was more noise behind the door, and then the knob began to turn. I ran down the stairs.

Uncle Jack was no longer asleep when I reached the ground floor, instead standing with his back to me, looking out of the window. "He's just trying to do what's best, you know?" he said, staring out at the night. He didn't turn to face me, as if he was watching the evening sky fade to black outside. "He's just trying to stop them. He's not a bad boy." As he turned to face me I saw the sadness etched in his face, but before I could respond there was a noise outside, the sound of a shotgun blast. My uncle screamed, stumbled back into his chair, and I ducked. A second shot rang out, and I realised neither had hit the house. I made sure my uncle was well away from the window, then crept to the door and slipped it open a crack. A cool wind swept in, carrying with it a distant noise of fighting. A scream. Another shotgun blast. The shot was accompanied by a brief flash. In that moment I saw the old man facing off against a tall dark figure amongst the trees, its frame obscured by fur or clothing that seemed to hang in, yes, tatters; the flash of a metal blade at the end of its arm.

My eyes adjusted to the darkness, as I saw the old man stumble to one knee. Rushing to his side, desperately hoping to help him fight off the terror that was attacking, I realised I could barely see in the gloom, couldn't see where the figure was any more. The old man, struggling to rise from the ground and fell into my arms, gun slipping from his hands. Wet. Warm. His shirt was slick with blood, a wound just below the ribs emptying his insides out. He rolled his eyes towards me as he struggled to speak. "Fucking bastard..." he exclaimed between gritted teeth, desperately struggling to get to his feet but only succeeding in kicking out wildly. He raised a bloodied hand and pointed, in the direction I had last seen the creature. I leaned in close, trying to lie him down, to hear what he wanted to say, as he drew in a painful breath to speak, but then he shuddered and spluttered and fell, a dead weight in my arms.

The forest was still. As the old man slipped from my grasp, onto the grass, I looked out, at the dark boundary where the trees lined the garden's edge, and saw nothing. And then, only when I suspected I must already be alone, did I see movement. A curved blade in the void. Lights from the house reflected momentarily in two circles. And then they vanished. I heard it, running, thinking first that it must be trying to outflank me, before it became apparent that it was running away.

I picked up the old man's shotgun. Not sure of what I would find, but determined to find answers, I followed the creature into the darkness, pursuing the noise as it crashed through the undergrowth. I guessed the old man had wounded it, perhaps had hit it several times, because it abandoned any attempts to hide itself. My previous experience with the Tattergaunt had suggested it was stealthy and silent, but there was none of that now. I ran, pushing aside branches as I had only days before, but this time in pursuit. So focused was I on following the noise that I didn't see the biker until his face loomed out of the darkness at me, as I pushed my way through the undergrowth.

I fell backwards, thinking that I was being attacked, shotgun raised to fire at him. The biker's mouth was agape, and for a moment I thought he was wearing goggles, perfectly round black circles covering his eyes, until I noticed the tears of blood that spilled down his face. He gazed at me, as much as a man without eyes can. It took me a few moments more to realise that he was also a man without a body. Where I had assumed the details of his biker leathers were lost in the shadows I suddenly comprehended as the empty space between trees, occupied only by tall dark spike upon which his head was impaled.

I backed away, screaming, pulling myself to my feet and then casting a glance around in case the Tattergaunt take advantage of my confusion. And moments later I saw something, movement from behind a nearby tree. I raised the shotgun once more, but the figure didn't move. Now that I had stopped scrambling in the dirt I could hear it faintly, above the stirring of leaves, a low moaning noise. A zombie? Not wanting to approach, knowing that one bite from one of those creatures would spell the end for me, I let my eyes adjust to the darkness, until I could make out that the figure was tied to the tree, neck straining as it tilted its head to look my way. In the darkness it took me a few moments more to recognise this figure as the second of the old man's companions. Still alive, but in a bad way.

His eyes, too, were gone. He struggled to speak, but I suspected his tongue had also been removed. Both arms were bound to the trunk of the tree but one hand was missing, severed just below the wrist. He can hear me, I realised. He can't do anything, can't say anything, but he can hear me. The man began to shake, struggling at his bonds. What the fuck was I supposed to do? Bring him back to the house? Put him out of his misery? Leave him? I could only imagine what he was thinking, could only imagine what's he was unable to say. Did he know who I was? Did he think I was his salvation? Or his doom?

A twig cracked behind me.

I spun around. A tall dark figure loomed right behind me, too close to discern where it ended and the surrounding darkness began. Until the shotgun I held exploded into life.

The figure shuddered, folding around the blast of the shotgun, as if it was reaching forward to grasp me. In that brief flash of light the creature was rendered real, physical, smaller, its shadow cast across the trees around it. Light reflected back at me from the perfectly round lenses of the goggles over its face.

Over his face.

Almost instantly I heard the muffled screams of pain, as the black shape crumpled to the ground, a tangle of limbs amongst a tattered cloak. Gloved hands struggled with the goggles and then the featureless black mask beneath it, but I already knew it was Peter. As he faced skywards, his skin catching the ambient light of the night sky, I recognised his features amongst the streaks of blood. "I'm sorry," he said, eyes finding mine, "I should've told you." I knelt down beside him, supporting his head, as he gasped out his apology. "I had to keep them away. Like the humans keep the orcs away. I had to keep them away!"

I tried to comfort him, tried to calm him, even as I struggled to understand why he'd do such a thing, but his next words answered much more than I ever imagined. "What do you do," he asked, "when the dead come back? What do you do when someone you love, someone you believe has been lost to you forever, comes back?" As tears started to clear faint trails across his bloody cheeks he continued, his voice cracking. "How do you keep them safe? How do you keep them safe when they come back changed? How?" He didn't say much more. He shook in my arms, crying for a moment, whilst I looked down at him. Finally he stopped shaking, his face relaxed. Peaceful.

I brought Peter back to the house with me. The rest of the bodies left out there, where they lay. I don't even know where the biker's body was. The old man's other companion didn't survive either. You've heard my cousin's confession, or what there was of it, so it seems only right that you hear mine too. I found the knife Peter had been using in his guise at the Tattergaunt, and ended the bound man's life quickly. I'd never killed a man in cold blood before. I can't say it felt like a mercy, as his life's blood spilled over my hands. I'm still in shock, I guess.

This story is nearly ended. The sun has begun to rise and I can just make out, in the garden, the two small headstones rise out of the ground. My aunt and my younger cousin. I feel the pieces all begin to slip into place, the mystery of Andrew's room in the attic, and Peter's last words. Peter had created the Tattergaunt in order to keep people away, but what had he been so scared they'd discover? Had Andrew survived the virus and had been forced into hiding for fear that the townsfolk would find and kill him? Had they kept it a secret even from their mother? Had her nightmares, of her dead son sitting at the end of the bed, been real after all? It all seemed so unlikely and yet, horribly, it all made sense.

And what of that thing I saw that first night, when I ran and collapsed into my cousin's arms? That couldn't have been Peter. Had I simply allowed the horror stories from the town to get the better of me? Was it one of the local orc population?

Oh God. Had it been Andrew?

I needed to confirm my suspicions, needed to know what's been going on. I needed to know that Peter had good reason to do the terrible things he did. I needed to know what - or who - is in the attic room.

I needed to put my mind at rest before I went crazy.

This account then is what I know of the dark secrets of this family. Of the truth behind the legend of the Tattergaunt. And perhaps, should I not return from the attic, it will prove to be useful to someone else who later comes this way.

I'm so sorry.

***

I fold the paper up and look around for somewhere to conceal it. In the end I resort to putting it into a small bottle from the kitchen. I decide to bury it, not too deep, in the soil where Andrew supposedly lays. I don't trust that anything I leave in the house won't be discovered by its inhabitants. Or destroyed.

There's a certain poetic justice to leaving it in Andrew's grave, I figure.

I ascend to the attic to find the door open. Someone has unlocked it and left it open, though the room beyond is now in darkness. I wondered for the first time whether the door was locked to keep someone in, or someone out.

I pause but, hearing nothing, I take a step closer. Then another. Before I have reached the doorway, before I even glimpsed the edge of the bed within, I can sense that someone is sitting there, in the darkness. There's breathing, low, and soft. My hand reaches towards the light switch on the attic landing.

"Brother?" whispers a low and guttural voice. The voice is both familiar and yet distorted, human and inhuman. I feel unable to move, as if in the presence of something terrifying. There's a scratching at the back of my mind, a half remembered verse or expression. "Brother?" the voice asks again, a slightly different tilt to it lending it some emotion, some sense of concern, "Is that you?"

"I..." I struggle to speak. I shake my head. "Peter is dead..." My voice trails off. How do I even start this conversation?

There is a soft laugh from the darkened room before the voice replies. "I was dead once. I mean, I must've been. Why else would you bury something, unless it was dead?" I hear the sound of feet shuffling in the darkness, and reflectively take a step back. "I thought I'd lost you, brother..."

"I'm not your brother," I explain, taking another step back, hands raised. But even as I speak the final word I realise that it is not Andrew walking towards me. The figure is wearing a dress. I try to comprehend what's going on. Is that my aunt's dress?

As the figure steps forward, the light gradually catching its features, it smiles a terrifying smile, crooked fangs curved around the lips of a blackened and distorted face. And yet it is familiar. And I realise that all the memories I've carried since the world ended, all the beauty I've glimpsed in the stars as they shine down, all my gratitude that the innocent could drift away into peaceful slumber and not know the horror of this hellish post-apocalyptic nightmare, they're all illusions. And as these illusions crack, fragments raining down around me, my brain cries out in denial.

"Welcome home, brother," says my sister.

DEAD RECKONING
JOHN HOULIHAN

"I t's a pretty looking bauble, girl, I'll grant you that, but it's not worth shit. Tell you what, because I like your face," he grinned sardonically, "I'll give you a hundred creds for it. What do you say?"

The trader held the data crystal up to the sun, its multifaceted surface glistening. His pungent mix of stale booze and staler body odour made her nostrils twitch, but Reshka's face remained impassive.

"Well, what do you say, girl? Cat got your tongue? Come on, I haven't got all day." Impatience warred with avarice, tipping his hand.

"She don't talk Jacobsen, but reckon she's given you her answer," said Rasoul, smirking. Jacobsen's eyes slid down to where Reshka's middle figure had risen to its fullest extension.

"Why you little Orc bitch!"

"Don't be a dick," said Rasoul, his burly frame casting a shadow over the pair. "Pay her what it's worth. We're Changed, not stupid." Reshka's palm opened, her black fingers uncurling.

"Five hundred... " her eyebrow raised almost imperceptibly, "oh alright then, fifteen hundred and I'm robbing myself blind." She nodded, accepted the crumpled credits, and strode off without a backward glance.

The voice was calling to her again and soon she must answer, but not now, there were other things to attend to. She watered the blooms with the nutrient-meat solution she'd bought with a small part of the trader's money and they sucked in the liquid gratefully, sighing then producing small bursts of harmonious music as they drank deep. She smiled, her garden was growing, expanding, claiming back the parched soil, filling out the little niche she had carved here, away from the dead city, where nothing ever grew.

The visit to the trading post had unsettled her, such visits always did. She didn't like people, even her own kind like Rasoul, although he was okay she supposed in a burly, overprotective kind of way. She saw the way he looked at her sometimes.

The noise and bustle made her nervous, but it was necessary to go there, to buy or trade for the things she couldn't grow or find or steal - things like the power cells. She finished her watering and listened to the notes diminish as the blooms ended their song.

An echo of the voice seemed to carry to her in the stillness, calling, pleading, enticing, willing her to its side once again, but she was strong, she would resist... for now. She watched the sun sinking toward the horizon, the last rays glinting off the angles of the porch and the ornaments which decorated her humble little shack. Soon, she thought, as the first stars peeped out in the purple-azure evening, soon.

***

The jackalope buck's whiskers twitched as it scented the cool evening air, its eyes bright and alert, its long ears erect, ready to detect any danger. Around it, the colony sifted its way through the stringy grass and straggly soil which marked the invisible frontier between the badlands and the city's outer suburb. Suddenly the buck tensed, its powerful back legs thumping hard and the colony scattered, rocketing down the holes and entrances of its warren, a blur of fearful movement.

A chitterhawk glided low in a long skimming swoop and then climbed again, its claws full with a small struggling kit. It settled in a nearby tree where it fed the unfortunate creature in chunks to its chicks. All this she saw, without opening her eyes, all this she felt, without using her external senses, standing there on the frontier. The voice called to her again and she stepped over the boundary and felt the city's dark influence penetrate her like a wave.

***

Jacon peered through the range finder. The scattered group of zeds were lethargic, listless, but they were slap bang in the way.

"There's no path around I can see, we'll just have to go straight through. Recommend I terminate them, sir," he whispered over the com. Even though his helmet kept his words insulated from the external world, he couldn't quite shake the engrained habit, the habitual discipline of silence.

"Do it. Inform me when we're clear to move," came the succinct reply. Braylin was not one to waste words. Jacon glanced at the pressure gauge and then selected his first target. She - it - was a ragged, pale-skinned young woman with frayed blonde hair, shambling listlessly around a rubbish bin in a repeating pattern. It had probably been beautiful once, but it didn't pay to think of these things as human any more. He put his eye to the sight, squeezed and the pressure rifle whispered its silent death. The zed dropped, its head a pulpy ruin, the projectile passing clean through and out the other side, leaving a crimson spray on the wall. The other zeds, even those in close proximity, didn't pause in their shambling. One down, plenty more to go.

They made their camp that night on the first floor of an abandoned shopping mall, silent alarms rigged to warn of any encroaching zeds and dampers deployed to mask any outgoing sound. Jacon drew first watch and while the other members of the CRC team bedded down, he seated himself at a window. As the sun sank below the horizon, light seemed to be sucked out of the necropolis, shadows swelling, plunging the dead city into eternal cold, an eternal night. He couldn't quite suppress the full body shiver which overtook him.

The distortions hadn't been too severe so far. Their suits protected them to an extent, as did the cocktail of chemical suppressants bubbling in their bloodstreams. But nothing could keep it out entirely. They had made reasonable progress too, despite a couple of frustrating loops where they had walked through sections, only to find themselves right back where they started. Eschering they called it - the city seeming to remould and reconfigure itself as you went, so that sometimes you could hardly tell east from west or up from down. Disorientating as it was, it was only the first stage, the precursor to the dead city's full madness.

Not for the first time, he wondered why he still did this, why he needed to. But a man had to eat after all, and it paid so well, that one decent score and all his responsibilities would be met for another six months.

That was a long time, long enough to recover from any lingering symptoms and the CRC's medical care was second to none. This job would pay a big bounty too, a mega score, almost enough to never have to set foot inside one of these places again: some long lost AI that somebody wanted found. One more time, he told himself, one last payload and then I'm out.

But he already knew he'd be back. He craved the thrill of it, silently threading your way through a city that wanted to eat you alive.

Braylin had a device that would help cut through the maze and their taciturn commander had been here before, or so he said. Yet the further in they went, the worse it would get.

"Quiet enough for you?" a voice came from the dark, almost causing his bones to jump out of his skin.

"Fuck!" The words surprised him, in here you were quiet or you were dead. But it was just Vasquez, looming out of the shadows, grinning and punching him hard in the shoulder.

"'Sup man, you starting to go freaky?"

"No, just thinking, that's all."

"Dangerous habit, you don't want to indulge in too much of that. Specially here. Just keep your eyes on the prize, man. When we get back you'll have all the time in the world to think, when you're a week-deep in some backstreet pleasure palace."
"Well, I'll be sure to write you... but I'll be sure to use only words with two syllables, I know you struggle with any more."

"Fuck you! That's only one syllable each."

"Ha, fuck you very much."

"Well, fuck you kindly." They both grinned again, easing the tension with a welter of profanity.

Suddenly Vasquez broke off, his expression turning serious as he pointed to a blinking sensor.

"Fuck, silent alarm, sector seven. Moving too quick for a zed. Wake the others, let's go check it out."

***

Reshka paused and her eyes flicked to the moon above. The city seemed to swallow its light and night stirred the possessed, made them more restless, rattling and moaning as they shuffled on

104

their eternal journey. She took a breath, steadied the weight of the backpack, then stepped lightly out across the top of the covered walkway, which screened her from the horde below. They didn't looked up, they never did, their collective gaze fixed on something far beyond the confines of this world.

She padded along noiselessly, like a great cat balancing her load, but when she came to the window, she seemed to have arrived at a different place entirely and now she was staring at a blank, very solid wall.

But it was just one of the city's many tricks and instinct guided her true. She put a hand out and the bricks seemed to part, dissolve and melt away and then reform into the shape of a window again. She stepped through, careful not to knock her precious cargo and then dropped into the deserted upper floor of the mall. Despite the filth and detritus strewn across the floor it was a useful shortcut; and it was only very rarely that one of the possessed meandered in here, perhaps driven by some half forgotten consumer instinct. There was nothing worth buying now, nothing in this place worth anything at all.

She padded along the upper tier confidently, though she was careful not to let her soft boots crunch the broken glass. Any sudden sound would draw even the most lethargic possessed like pins to a magnet, transforming them from indolent shuffling statues to raging fury in an instant.

The long corridor ahead of her suddenly twisted and elongated, becoming distorted and full of towering, shadowy figures. The dead city again, trying to deceive her, it was like a game that it played against her, but she trusted herself and her purpose held true. She hefted the weight of the backpack and walked calmly through the hallucination, ignoring the pair of shadowy demons which detached themselves from the pack, studiously ignored their gibbering, right up until the moment a very solid and very real rifle barrel was pressed directly against her temple. She froze.

"Shit girl, what the fuck are you doing here?" A voice whispered and now the demons became human figures, two men, heavily armed, and wearing tactical combat suits.

"Answer me or I will shoot you where you stand," one of them hissed, his eyes darting beyond her.

"Easy Vasquez, easy. She's just a girl," the other figure whispered.

"She's an Orc, and if she cries out, she'll bring a screaming horde down on our heads. So I'll say again, what you the fuck are you doing here, girl? Answer me, *now*."

Reshka pointed to her throat and shook her head.

"Fuck's that? What the fuck's that mean?"

"I think she's saying she can't speak." Reshka nodded at the other.

"Can't or won't?"

"I don't know, but let's not debate it here. Let's get her back to the quiet zone. We can question her properly there."

"Okay girl, you're coming with us. But make a sound or try and run for it, and you'll be measuring your length on that floor before you can take another step. Understand?" Reshka nodded and then the unyielding barrel prodded her hard in the back and they moved off into the shadows.

***

"We're coming in," she heard the younger one say, as they passed the glowing outer markers. They walked forward and her two captors stowed their weapons and held their palms open. A ring of men greeted them, similarly armed and armoured, gripping their rifles. But as her captors were recognised, the men relaxed and several barrels dropped a notch.

"What have you got there, Jacon?" A grizzled, grey-haired man with an eye patch strode forward and regarded her sternly.

"We found her wandering through the upper storey of the mall, Commander, tootling along as if she didn't have a care in the world."

"Why did you bring her back Jacon? This is an extraction mission, we're not here to rescue stray damsels in distress." There were a few sour laughs and a few curses.

"Thought it best. Wouldn't do to have a stray rubble monkey wondering around this close to our position." The older man considered this for a moment, but his gaze never left her.

"Smart. What's your name girl? What are you doing here?" Braylin's single orb bored into her.

"She mute, sir, doesn't speak as far as we can tell," said Vasquez. Braylin took this news with obvious displeasure. "Well, she's little use to us then. If... "

Reshka's hands began to move, fingers weaving to form the words.

"What's she doing now?"

"I think it's sign language, sir," said Jacon. "My sister was deaf, let me see if I can... yeah it's ASL American standard, just give me a moment... "

I am Reshka... a... wanderer... a traveller. Jacon translated.

"Wandering around a dead city," growled Braylin. "Are you touched? You're not safe here."

This is my city. You're the ones who aren't safe.

"Fuck, well she has a sense of humour at least," said the commander, "but we don't have room for passengers and we can't just set her loose." He drew his sidearm meaningfully. Jacon looked appalled, but the girl's fingers whirred again,

What is it you seek? I know the ways of the city well, its many paths, its many traps, its many deceptions. Perhaps I can help you?

"Do you know the Atlanta building?" said Jacon quickly, but Reshka's expression remained blank. "A tower block with four spires, like this... " he drew a crude picture in the dust.

A strange look passed across her impassive features but then she nodded curtly.

Fallen, dangerous, many possessed.

"Possessed?"

"I think she means the zeds, sir."

"Hm, yeah well we know all about them girl, but the prize is worth the risk," said Braylin.

Prize?

"An AI, an artificial mind, buried somewhere deep in that tower, that's what we're after. But don't you worry your head about that, just get us close and we'll do the rest. Afterwards, we'll reward you, give you credits, many credits."

How many?

"Ha, that's more like it. More than you could ever spend."

I will take you there. But it will not be easy.

"It never is girl, but we have weapons, equipment, tech, enough gear to cover any eventuality."

Deal.

"Jacon, Vasquez, congratulations, you're now in charge of our new guide. Find her a place to bed down. We move early, but if she tries to leave, shoot her. Understood?"

"Aw, Commander I... "

Braylin's eye narrowed.

"Problem Vasquez? I'm not used to repeating myself. Is something I said unclear to you?"

"No sir, all as clear as day," said Vasquez, but his face told a different story.

***

Screaming, he clawed away the ring of dead, dead eyes and dead, dead faces as they hemmed him in. Desperate, frantic, he beat his fists to bloody ruins as he tried to hold back the inevitable.

Jacon woke with a start, but all was quiet. The girl sat cross-legged a couple of metres away, eyes staring outward, as if communing with something in the beyond. His movement shook her from her reverie and she turned to look at him, her full black eyes shining like mirrors.

You should leave now. She signed. *There is only death here.*

"Good morning to you too."

I am sorry, I should thank you. Your commander would have shot me without your intervention.

"My pleasure, answer me something in return. Why do you come here?"

I have no choice. I must.

"Must? No one has to stalk a dead city without good reason. Why aren't you dead or crazy like the rest?"

Perhaps I am.

"You seem sane enough to me."

Sane enough for a Changed... an Orc?

"I don't see Changed, or an Orc, I see a girl."

What I am doesn't matter. Death is coming, it will take them all. You should go, now, leave the others, save yourself.

"What's she saying?" interrupted Vasquez brusquely.

"She wants to know if there's any breakfast, that's all," Jacon lied.

"Well tell her to eat hearty," said Vasquez slapping a ration pack down. "If we're going to have to nursemaid her through the rest of this damn day, I don't want to stop to have her feed her face every five minutes." Reshka looked at the pack, but didn't move.

"Saddle up. We move in ten. No exceptions." Braylin said.

Reshka nodded, but her dark eyes never left Jacon.

***

She was good. It didn't take him long to realise that. Far from having to nursemaid her, Reshka led them efficiently and decisively, having an instinctive feel for the highways and byways of the dead city and seemingly immune from its many lethal distractions. As the city's streets and avenues folded and remoulded themselves before their eyes, she held her course, unerring and true.

Scuttling between the shadows cast by the concrete skeletons of the ruined metropolis, they snatched hurried glimpses of the Atlanta's distinctive spires and by midday, it had drawn appreciably closer.

Reshka also seemed to possess an uncanny knack for evading the zeds, naturally, Jacon supposed or she wouldn't have lasted five minutes in here. Those they couldn't find a way around, she spotted before the creatures detected them and then directed Jacon and Vasquez's pressure rifles which cut a silent, deadly swathe through the creatures.

They arrived at the intersection sometime near mid-afternoon, a bubbling, viscous heat shimmering on the broken tarmac and uncharacteristically, the girl halted, staring at the sky, scenting the air, as if she were entranced by a sound beyond their hearing. She stayed like that for several minutes, immobile, immune to their promptings, even when Vasquez shook her. Soon, Braylin and the others had caught up and were at their side. The sky began to darken and a sullen breeze sprang up.

"What's wrong?" said the commander.

"Search me. Looks like someone's hit her off switch."

Reshka's eyes cleared and she turned to Jacon.

The demon. The demon comes. She signed.

"The what?" demanded Braylin, when Jacon relayed it to him.

We need to hide, now! she signed tugging at Jacon's arm.

Now the unnatural stillness began to swirl, gathering itself like wrath. The CRC team muttered to themselves, looking around anxiously.

This way, this way. Reshka signed and darted toward the remnant of an old subway entrance, waving them to follow.

Quickly, quickly, the demon comes!

Jacon was already inching toward her and now the rest looked to Braylin. The wind started to tear at their faces, the sky howling.

"Follow her, find cover!" shouted Braylin and they stormed over to the entranceway, piling down the steps in a frantic rush. The space below was dark and smelled of rot and decay. They huddled nervously together on the landing.

Do not look. Do not look directly at it. She signed, screwing her eyes shut and covering her ears. The rest of them obeyed but Jacon couldn't quite help himself. As the monstrous shrieking above them neared a crescendo, he peeped around the corner, using just his peripheral vision.

The thing blotted out the daylight. He registered a primordial, swirling ball of chaos, an unholy maelstrom lit from within by flashes of purple lightning. He had a fleeting impression of surging tendrils, thousands of flashing eyes, distorted unnatural limbs, all forming and reforming within its unclean mass. His eyes snapped shut as a wave of hopelessness, of profound alienation engulfed him. The very air seemed to drown him, and he found his gun rising, an inexorable urge to jam it in his mouth and pull the trigger overcoming him; to end the eternal horror which held him like a palpable thing.

But then a firm hand gripped his own, and when he looked again, Reshka's deep black sclera-less eyes were locked on his own. Moments passed and then the urge started to drain away and he was himself again. Distantly, those terrible shrieks and howls died away, as the demon surged elsewhere.

But it had not left them unscathed. Two of the CRC team lay dead by their own hands. One had used his rifle to blow his brains out, the other had taken a knife and slit his own throat, a long stream of crimson spilling down his body armour.

"Shit, what the fuck was that?" demanded Vasquez.

The demon. It is his city too. I warned you of the danger.

"You did. Well, reckon we should thank you anyway, girl," said Braylin. "You saved us. Well, most of us, anyway."

Reshka nodded, but signed nothing else.

***

The spires of the Atlanta building loomed over them, as they watched from the shelter of a dilapidated car park. They were close enough to take a simple thirty second stroll to its main entrance, and they would have, had it not been for the swarm of intervening zeds that lay between them and their goal. The creatures were agitated and restless, groaning and colliding with each other, as if anticipating something.

"Fuck," whispered Braylin. "That's pissed in our cornflakes."

Perhaps the demon has called them? Maybe it seeks to deny you your prize?

"That's not helpful girl," said Braylin and they contemplated the swarm in silence.

There might be another way, but it is not an easy path to walk.

"Show us."

Ten minutes later found them overlooking a second entrance on the eastern side of the tower. The zeds were slightly less numerous here, but there were still perhaps a couple of hundred, circling on their endless march.

"How is this any better?"

You said if I got you close, you would do the rest. This is as close as we get.

They regarded the intervening space. Half way between their elevated position and the entrance, four giant figures, statues of an almost inhuman perfection, thrust a pedestal aloft by their raised arms, the platform bearing the remnant of some long-forgotten corporate symbol.

There, it could act as a bridge to get across. You have rope?

"We've got better than rope," said Vasquez. "The spider line. We could anchor it on the top of that platform then zipwire across. Once we're there, we retract, fire again and then go hand over hand into the building."

"Over a swarm of angry zeds?"

"If we're ultra-quiet, they shouldn't notice. It's probably our best chance of getting in there." Braylin's brow furrowed as he studied the problem.

"Very well. Make your preparations," said Braylin. "Jacon, you're on overwatch, you'll cover us from here."

"But- " Jacon started to protest. Braylin's raised eyebrow cut him off.

***

The spider line snaked silently across the thirty metre gap and then its hooks caught, biting into the surface of the elevated platform. Vasquez pulled it taught, tested its weight, then gave a thumbs-up. Braylin nodded, hooked in and launched himself down the line. He skimmed over the zeds, his harness making a whizzing sound and dropped lightly onto the raised surface. The CRC team watched intently, waiting for any reaction, but the zeds didn't stir, didn't even seem to notice. Grins all round.

One by one the remaining half dozen members of the team followed, Reshka taking the penultimate ride, followed by Vasquez, until they all stood there, above the sea of shambling corpses. Vasquez retracted the line and its rear head whistled across the gap and then locked into the launcher. Reshka pointed to a ledge on one of the lower floors where some of the windows stood open.

"Reckon you can make the shot, Vasquez?" said Braylin over the com.

"Piece of cake, sir," he said, already lining up the launcher's sights. Jacon watched as the hook shot out again and embedded itself into the concrete of the tower, and then Vasquez re-anchored the line. Reshka stepped up, ready to try the rope, but Braylin held her back, indicating she should wait, then pointed at Vasquez. He tested the line once again with a tug and then jumped up and went hand over hand, swarming across the intervening gap, until he stood on the ledge of the building.

Braylin pointed at Reshka, indicating it was her turn and the girl hefted her backpack and soon made short work of it, her lithe, black, muscular body bridging the distance with ease. Soon she was next to Vasquez on the ledge and Jacon's gaze flicked back to the group in the centre. Now Braylin grasped the line and made ready to ascend, but then he stopped, shouting over the com.

"Fuck! What are you doing girl!?"

Jacon quickly scoped back to the ledge. Vasquez teetered there, a stream of crimson running down from his knee and over his boot. As he clawed at the wound, he was given a violent shove and fell screaming onto the concrete steps ten metres below. The nearest zeds jolted like they'd been shocked, suddenly swarming toward him. He shrieked and thrashed as a biting, rending wave engulfed him.

Stunned, Jacon scoped back to see Reshka hacking through the spider line, severing its head with a knife. The broken line fell limply into the space below. She hopped quickly through one of the open windows as a hail of bullets peppered the spot where she had just stood. Jacon could see her inside now, standing back but framed by the window. She was now out of sight of the others, but seemed to know he was watching her. She signed.

They are doomed. Save yourself.

Then she was gone, disappearing into the bowels of the building as if she had never existed. Now Jacon could hear oaths, curses and worse echo over the com. Without its head, the spider line was useless, and there was no way to retrieve it now, Braylin and the rest were stranded there on an island amidst a sea of dead.

Worse, their shots had drawn the attention of the horde. Jacon and Vasquez's pressure rifles were the only truly silent weapons, but even the dull retorts of the CRC team's silenced SMGs, had been enough to stir the creatures. Dozens were now milling around the base of the platform, snapping and clawing, piling over each other in their eagerness to infect the living. Braylin and the others started firing, desperately mowing down dozens of the creatures. Bullet cases rattled the platform, but in the short space it took each member to reload and change their magazine, the horde gained a little ground.

Vasquez's cries had long since ceased but now his twitching, lurching corpse rose and suddenly sprinted, hurling itself toward the beleaguered team. The zeds were high enough to spill over the edge of the platform now, and Braylin and his men were firing at point blank range, then using their weapons like clubs to batter the creatures away.

But it was no use, there was a sudden push and the swarm surged over them like the tide at high water. Jacon looked away as their screams filled the com channel, but soon there was nothing but silence.

***

"Reshka! You've come. I am humbled."

"I have brought the power cells you need to sustain you, Sebastian."

"Oh, marvellous, you are a positive delight my girl. Any problems getting through this time?"

"A few, the demon was abroad, but I managed to evade it."

"Well done."

"Also: some foolish men came, they wished to take you away, remove you from this place."

"Me? Why would they wish to take me?"

"For your knowledge I suppose."

"I see, what happened to them?"

"The city took them."

"A tragedy. A real tragedy, but the city is so full of them. Tell me, were you able to speak to them, warn them at all?"

"One was able to sign, I tried, but the rest would not listen."

"I see, I see. Well you did your best I suppose and that is all anyone can ask."

"It is."

"Tell me Reshka, why will you not talk out loud to anyone except me?"

"I have nothing to say to anyone else," she said, aligning the power cell in its socket. The AI's artificial face became brighter.

"Ah, thank you Reshka, that feels so much better, I am renewed once again, thanks to your good graces."

"You are very welcome, Sebastian. Now, tell me again of the time before, the time before the Yellow Dawn... "

IN MEMORY OF DAVID J ROGER

FALL OF OPHIUCHUS
SAMANTHA J. RULE
& ELI JOHNSTON

Prologue

Cutting clean lines through the clear blue water, the *Jeləʊ Kɪŋz* made its way around the Attica peninsula under a bright afternoon sun. An ancient Beneteau Océanis 46, with a modified electric propulsion system replacing the original combustion engine, she shined when sailed using the original fractional sloop. Under full sail, while not fast by any measure, she was a delight to handle. One hand on the helm, a glass and metal trinket in the other, Eirin guided the ship by the feel of the wind across his cheek as it deflected off the mainsail. He had navigation systems, of course, but their use diminished the experience immeasurably. His passenger seemed content to lie on the bow deck and absorb the view.

In sight of a private resort beach, under the gaze of a couple stretched out on the sand watching the world over the tops of their toes, Eirin moored his ship. He and his passenger made the short swim to their destination, a steep landing at the bottom of the mountainous peninsula. Eirin's lanky stride took him up a stone pathway with ease, while her shorter legs carried her up the trail with some effort. The rocks upon which they trod were darkened and smoothed by the weather of countless centuries. The narrow path led them up, past the flattened remnants of an old civilization, to the temple perched atop. It was a broken crown of marble gleaming in the afternoon sun, set on a ruined skull of land jutting out of the sea; honour for a faded god. The sun, blazing a fearsome warning for all below, greeted his deeply bronzed skin. Freckles on hers were practically appearing before his eyes. The earth was long cracked in its dryness. The few scattered weeds bowed before the heat and offered meagre shade to a family of ορτύκι.

He stood for a time, the broken temple of the forgotten water god to his back, gazing out over the sea while loosely rolling his trinket about with his fingers. His reverie was interrupted by the sounds of small feet approaching from behind. A tremulous voice presently asked "Excuse me, do you have permission to be here?"

He turned and met the woman's question with his smile. Her name badge and uniform, generically official, designated her as a member of the Hellenic Ministry of Culture.

"The last time I was here no permission was needed." His companion looked quizzically at him but stayed silent.

"Sir," her voice had firmed now, "you must pay a fee and receive the proper documentation. If you'll come with me."

Eirin ignored her instructions and pulled a small green passport from his back pocket.

"Please look inside."

She took his passport and opened it, pulling out a small card that was tucked inside. As she reviewed it her eyes widened slightly.

"I'm so sorry to bother you," she said with a quaver in her voice, then turned and made her way hurriedly down the hill.

"I've heard stories about you." His companion said, maintaining her steady gaze .

Eirin returned the documents to his pocket. "The genius that melded psychology and electricity to his bidding?"

"That's an odd way of stating it, but yes."

Behind her the sky was turning shades of orange and pale violet over deepest blue. The wind came up off the water, catching her hair; refracted light turning it from dripping honey to dancing flame.

Eirin pointed to the cliff edge a few meters to their left. "Captain, did you know that a king leapt to his death right here? His son renamed the sea to honour him, and for many years after, seventy men and women would be sent into the water after him on the anniversary of his passing."

"Please don't call me Captain," she replied flatly. "And no. Was it recent?"

Eirin shook his head and continued, his inviting smile stretching even wider. "It was a while back. An old acquaintance wrote a verse or two about it. *Place me in Sunium's marbled steep, where nothing, save the waves and I, may hear our mutual murmurs sweep: there, swan like, let us sing and die.*"

He saw that her eyes had dropped to the trinket in his hand. He turned it over, the glass and metal flashing ribbons of reflected light.

"Would you like a closer look?"

"I've never seen anything like it. What does it do?"

"Consciousness, as you perceive it, is little more than an illusion created through the plasticity of your brains. Your minds, in effect, do not want you to see reality – they want you to see that which will allow you to exist long enough to continue the species."

Eirin gently placed the object in her hand. Static sparks flitted about her head. "You are used to imposture. I strip away illusion. I allow you to see reality."

The pastel sky retreated, as it always must, before the advance of darkness.

2276.001 – Shift Change

A calm wind rustled the crisp leaves of trees, and chimes gently danced. Happy flights of birds gave a rapid song to serve as counterpoint to this natural composition. These gentle sounds gradually gave way; first to the rippling of water, then to a magnetic hum, and finally rising to a harsh cacophony of metal colliding with metal while a fierce storm voiced outrage. First Officer Riley Carter awoke with a start, hands reaching and grasping at nothing, before she calmed and forced herself to take a deep breath. It was always the same, each time the wake-up protocol initiated, the same sequence of sounds played out in her head; a jarring experience on perpetual repeat.

Nanocarbon Synco brains were supposed to work exactly like real brains. In sensory translation, intellect, emotions, and even dreaming the Synco brains delivered what they promised. Mostly. A complex network of cyberware was installed in tandem to ensure smooth communications between a synthetic cortex and a genetically modified, mostly organic body. However, nothing felt less organic than waking up after a period of synthetic deep sleep. Nothing at all like her transferred memories of what it was like to wake up with a brain native to the consciousness within it.

Her eyes quickly gained focus and landed upon the face of her commander and co-pilot, Jian Lau. He was peering at her through the glass and rapping his knuckles against the cryotank.

"Wakey wakey, eggs and bakey! Well as far as eggs and bacon go on this junker. Am I right, Carter?" He turned and continued down the semi-circular line to wake the other half of the crew for the shift changeover.

The computer chirped inside her tank before spouting off the medical stats of her body's vitals post-thaw; the temperature of her synthetic blood, the structural integrity of her cellular walls, and the operational capacity of her 3D printed organs. She punched a button on the wall for the shower. A warm mist, smelling of clinical sanitizer, washed over her. She rubbed her chilled hands across her face and groaned with a voice of smoke. "Here we go again."

And so went the changing of watch on the interstellar craft *Shé Chengzai*. Every twelve months, local time, the sitting command crew would wake up their shift replacements, bring them up to date with a SitRep, and then take their turn in deep sleep. Seventy years of standard time, broken into forty shift rotations, would mark the imminent arrival of humanity, both to exoplanet Wolf 1061c and as a multi-solar species.

2276.002 – First Day of Duty

Riley Carter made her way from crew quarters to the *Shé Chengzai's* centrally located control room. Bioluminescent algae lined the terrarium walls, washing her face with a gentle cyan that barely registered in the visible light spectrum. Riley's Nano Retinas translated the near-darkness into a starkly lit reality, and her osseointegrated vibratory stimulator allowed her to perceive the inaudible trickle of water coming from the recycling and filtration system inside the walls. Every square centimetre of the ship had a purpose, and most resources served multiple; algae provided a source of light, oxygen, and nutritional supplement all in one functional bioengineered package.

Data screens splashed colour through the hatchway, a festive parade of red and blue greeting her arrival. Riley strapped herself in at her station and took in the scattered array of information waiting for her review.

"Ek'aro, Riley!"

Chief Engineer Jonathan Adeyemi had entered the room behind her. Nigerian born, he was a compact man who always had a clean-shaven head and a broad smile on his face. During zero-g training he had looked comical, a gleeful delight on his face as he floated around in his jumpsuit.

"Did you enjoy your nap?" Riley asked, her fingers twitched reflexively as her security code initiated and unlocked holographic displays for the command consoles throughout the ship.

"I had this incredible dream about my wife. She was taking her clothes off in the kitchen and then --"

"Oh no! I've heard enough, thank you." Riley stopped him before he could continue, turning back to her holo-display. "I'm sure the real Jonathan Adeyemi loved the idea of sharing all of his memories with a carbon copy. Seriously, I don't blame the guy for never letting his wife visit while we were around."

"Kini?" He snorted indignantly. "You're just jealous that your original didn't have a special someone to share in your dreams. You can't blame me for having a wife while you were alone. Kindly keep your sour grapes to yourself."

"You've got me all figured out, haven't you?" Riley asked flatly. She went through her checklist silently. She could now see crewmembers on the ship logging in at their stations. A ding sounded as the medical officer registered in the medical bay. Another chimed in as Jonathan's login appeared on her screen as well. He cleared his throat.

"You know, I don't like it when you say that." His voice broke the silence.

"What, carbon copy?"

"Yes."

"Well, that's what we are, isn't it?"

"I know, but I still don't like it."

Gods help me. Riley took a deep breath and released it slowly. "Look, I'm sorry, Jonathan."

Silence was her only answer. A myriad of system displays sprang into her vision like a blooming flower of fireworks; a master panel of systems controls on ocular display. Crew vitals showed normal in all cryotanks. The stasis of the foetal colonists was within normal parameters. The ship's QG system was nominal. The shielding seemed fine, although a maintenance reminder popped up on screen. Atmospheric module normal as well. A small blue icon pulsed in a corner, unopened communications in her personal inbox via the QEComm relays.

Adeyemi's hands swiped in the air over his displays, cycling through his roster of systems checks. "If you'll excuse me, I have my rounds to make. Apparently, the toilets aren't working." He sighed in disgust.

"Aren't the mechs supposed to be doing that?"

He stood abruptly. "Some of them are pinging back under 80%. Knowing Adams, he probably slacked on their preventative maintenance. Now I get to fix mechs and clean up shit!"

The blue icon continued flashing in the corner of her screen.

"It's a splendid job we have." Riley beamed him a cheeky smile. "Keeping the machines running that keep the machines running. Speaking of upkeep, will you have them run a check on the shields?"

"Sure thing. Just call if you need something else." He waved a hand dismissively before ambling out of the room.

Riley waited until he was gone and then turned her attention back to the pulsing blue icon, hesitating a moment. Her hand edged closer to the holographic display until she felt the buzz from the haptic response of her touch. Communications opened.

The first message came from the Athanasia Initiative, based in an orbital facility around Earth's paraterraformed moon. A private contractor, they were one of several groups developing deep space exploration and human colonization. While other groups were advancing research in UAV's and mechanoids, the Initiative sought to advance humanity through genetic engineering. Interstellar space travel was still out of reach for flesh evolved for life in the safety of a gravity well, but the Initiative had developed a fabrication process that allowed the fashioning of stronger organic bodies that withstood the damage inherent in deep space travel. The keystone of their work was a method of copying and transferring minds to new bodies without killing the original brain in the process. A closely guarded secret, very few knew how they achieved it and no other group or government had duplicated the process successfully. Partnered with the multi-state bloc that underwrote the *Shé Chengzai,* the Initiative fashioned the crew that would take the ship to the heart of the Ophiuchus constellation.

Riley started the message. The face that appeared on the screen wasn't what she was expecting. She was expecting to be greeted by her own visage, by the original Riley Carter, who worked at Initiative's control centre. What greeted her instead was the grinning face of a thin, swarthy man with sable coloured eyes.

His voice was dry, like a hot desert wind. "Good morning, First Officer Carter. I'm Doctor Dubhghall with the Athanasia Initiative." He adjusted in his seat. His body moving while his head remained impossibly fixed; a predator gazing at prey. "Captain Carter is out for a day or two, so I'll be filling in for her on this end." He smiled, awkward and thin-lipped. Riley found the overall picture to be disconcerting. The hairs on the nape of her neck stood up as if she'd caught sight of a spider at the edge of her vision. "When you are on duty and have completed your checks, please contact me at your earliest convenience. I will await your reply." The video terminated.

Somewhat unnerved, Riley deleted the message and selected the next unopened one. She certainly wasn't in a hurry to contact her temporary liaison at the Initiative. The second message was from Commander Lau. He appeared on screen, a figure drawn mostly from shadows and illuminated faintly by the instrument panel and dull green from the walls. His face looked balmy with sweat, which was odd considering the ship maintained a chilly atmosphere despite its layers of shielding and insulation. His breathing was shallow and rushed, as he kept peeking over his shoulder as if expecting to find something there.

"Seventy cycles," the commander said in hushed tones. "We must descend seventy cycles of cold dreaming before we can bask in the warmth of our new sun. At least, that's what he whispers to me while I'm sleeping." He rubbed his fingers against his furrowed brow. "I thought I was crazy at first. Then I thought maybe it was Him that was crazy. But He's been showing me things. I've seen our future settlements! Our beautiful cities of marble and gold set ablaze in the setting sun. It's a poetry of destruction." He nervously laughed as if he was forcing himself. "I just don't know what to think. I still haven't told the Initiative, or anyone else onboard. But I wanted someone to know. I wanted you to know, Carter. I've been talking to a psych doctor they brought in. I don't talk about the dreams though. He's quite interesting, always going off on tangents about psychology and technology. I think they're worried that Colonel Lau's latent instability transferred over. Who could have guessed that the guy was going to crack, huh? At any rate, I trust that you'll keep an eye on me. I'll see you next cycle."

The video went black.

Completely bonkers, and we're not even halfway there. Riley deleted the commander's message and ran sweeps through the cached files to ensure its complete removal. A ding sounded, Jonathan was logged in at the maintenance bay. Riley's view of his workstation panel showed the command prompts he entered for the system to check the programming for the shields. Riley could easily imagine him grumping up a storm as he pulled the mechs off the line, one by one, to run maintenance on them. She turned her attention to the crew in cryo, glancing at Commander Lau's stats. She buzzed through internal comms to the medical bay.

"How's it going down there, Doctor Bachchan?"

"Right as rain, Riley," the medical officer answered cheerily through the holo-display. "All tucked into bed and quietly in delta sleep. Hey, its first day on duty. You're cooking dinner, right?"

"Why am I always the first to cook?" Riley laughed.

"You've got to, um, lead by example!" Chandra Bachchan countered.

"Fine, fine, you talked me into it. How's Thai curry rice balls sound?"

"Ugh, why is it always curry with you?"

"I find the spice assortment perfect for masking that disgusting tofu, thank you very much. Before dinner, I've got to get on the QEComms with AI and touch base."

"Ooh, exciting. Have fun with that." Chandra made no effort to hide her sarcasm. "I want you to file a formal complaint while you're at it. Tell them that having us grow their colonists like sea-monkeys on arrival don't constitute parenthood. There better be a chemi-surgeon among the colonists' Syncos that will reverse our infertility. I'd like to take part in populating a new colony if it's not too much to ask. Anyways, I'll see you later, Riley." Chandra flippantly threw a hand up dismissing the comm and the view of the medical bay blinked out.

Riley initiated the QEComm and connected through to the Initiative. There was an empty chair on the other side.

"This is First Officer Carter of the *Shé Chengzai* checking in."

She could hear movement off-screen, and then Doctor Dubhghall stepped into view and sat down. Riley fingers twitched nervously, unnoticed, on the console.

"We appreciate you checking in, Carter. I don't believe I've had the pleasure to speak with you yet. How is everything going?" The doctor held a transparent tablet in one hand with a stylus at the ready for notations in the other.

"Well, everything seems to be going smoothly," Riley's shoulders shrugged against the belted restraints. "Our rate of travel is on schedule, and all ship systems are normal."

"I wasn't inquiring about the parameters of the mission, Carter, I was inquiring about you."

"I feel fine." Something about him made her uneasy. Why wasn't Captain Carter available for her to speak to today? "I haven't noticed anything out of the ordinary on duty or in cryo, either. I'd say all functions normal there as well."

"What about the crew?"

"A little wear-and-tear fatigue which is to be expected considering the length of the mission, but overall everyone seems to be maintaining an even keel." Her eyes wandered away from the QEComm screen to the external cameras. The Orion Nebula grew fainter each time she woke up from cryo as the *Shé Chengzai* moved farther away from it. Soon, her artificial photoreceptors wouldn't be able to detect the nebula's pink and blue hues, it would just be black.

"And what about the commander?" he asked.

"I would say the same for him." Her attention snapped back to him.

The stylus paused, and he peered up at her with a piercing glance. "Should you observe any abnormalities in anyone's behaviour, the Athanasia Initiative asks that you inform us immediately."

"Of course, Doctor. Was there anything else you needed to discuss?" She hoped to wrap this up before he could continue his very direct line of questioning.

"Thank you, that will be all for now. We'll be in touch." His discomfiting gaze dropped as more notations were written down. Riley terminated the communication and exhaled a deep sigh before scrolling through newsfeeds from Earth. It looked bad. Waves of riots were rocking most major Western cities. While power had shifted peacefully to Asia nearly two centuries ago, most Western powers had prepared enough to have varying degrees of economic soft landings. Headed by an enigmatic Egyptian ruler, the recent and rapid rise of the African Union had sent shockwaves through the global economy and put many European and American nations on the edge of economic ruin. Radical leaders spoke of impending battles against the blackness and destruction of ultimate space. This was going to be a long year.

2277.001 – Shift Change

Riley marvelled at how Jian Lau appeared to be pulling it all together. She had felt increasingly nervous over the past year, as the Captain's VidComm message had replayed in her mind. Despite the strict time schedule of regular changeovers, she had observed him closely enough to feel comfortable that he was fit for another – the final – year of command. He had perfectly handled their midpoint manoeuvre years ago, and would also handle to final deceleration as they entered their destination system.

The new shift had been awake for a few hours, and Captain Lau was already at his station. The computer chimed in multiple successions with each crewmember logging on/checking in at their stations.

The ship had some minor damage spots – forty years local time of gliding and colliding through the dust and debris of space. He quickly reviewed the damage and the order list; Riley had made sure mechs were already fabricating replacement parts to be installed by the new shift. As he went through his checklist Riley took the opportunity to talk.

"Those are some pretty dark circles you're sporting there, Captain."

"A whole year, and that's what you're going to say to me?" There was an odd glint in his eyes as he peered over at her. He looked exhausted and energized at the same time.

"How do you feel? You left quite the message for me last cycle."

"That's right, I'd forgotten." His eyes drifted downwards and his fingers went still. "I felt fine most days, but sometimes I just didn't feel like myself. A strange disassociation but how can we not feel that way? Being what we are? Considering where we are?"

"You're still not convinced humanity was meant to traverse the stars, are you?"

"Perhaps," he mused for a moment in silence. "What an experience though, right?"

"And responsibility. What's your news from the Initiative?" Riley asked quietly.

Jian glanced around furtively before answering, "My original. He's dead."

Riley sucked in a breath; muscles tense, waiting for the rest of it.

"He was getting delirious last year, having hallucinations. He kept talking about dreams, and about how he was supposed to leave. He kept leaving me messages advising me to talk to Dr Dubhghall, he said he was meeting with him regularly and had seen things he couldn't believe." Jian's skin had taken on a waxy, sickly sheen. "The message says he went into a subway station and threw himself in front of a maglev. There's another message from him, he must have left it right before. I stopped it a few seconds in – it was just mad talk, trackless snow sweeping the world aside to make way for gleaming columns of light et cetera."

Riley was aghast. "I am sorry about your original. You two seemed to get along quite well."

"I'll be fine." He spat the words out. "He may have lost his way, but I know my purpose."

"What a glorious burden, eh?"

"Yeah, sure. So what about you? How's your original doing? The news feed I'm getting now looks really grim - it all seems to be falling apart back there."

"We haven't talked in a while. She was trying to convert me to some new religion that's spreading across northern Africa and the Arabian Peninsula. She's also been undergoing biomech enhancement surgery. A lot. Every time we talk she has a new prosthetic, and she just wants to talk about how alive it makes her feel and yet how she's exactly the same as always."

Jian's visage became severe. "We've come so far, we can't fail now. You understand, don't you, Carter?"

He turned his piercing gaze towards her, his features somehow transformed by the darkening of his mood.

"Yes, I understand."

They spent the rest of the day in near silence as the Captain resumed full control of the ship. When it was time, he walked with her to her cryotank. Riley settled in, exhausted by the sombre mood of the day.

Jian closed her tank and then stood with his hands at the controls, a grim tightness at the corners of his mouth. "I don't think the Initiative quite understands what they've done, or where they're sending us. There is a hand behind the scenes, pulling the strings."

"Who is pulling the strings?"

His eyes were black. "*He* is. He's the dark of the universe containing all of its stars and celestial bodies. Carrying us in this silent blackness."

Quiet alarm coursed through Riley. "And what does He want from us?"

"We're going to build His new kingdom with our colony."

As Riley drew in a breath to reply, the drugs already in her system took hold.

Captain Jian leaned over her tank. "Don't worry. I've never felt better."

XXXX.XXX – Shift Change

Perched at the bow of a black-clad ship of the sea, Riley's heart jumped at the sight of the Attica peninsula as it rose out of the distant water, topped with columns of fiery yellow and orange blazing towards the sun-drenched sky. Carrion birds circled lazily overhead as she sailed towards the chime of copper bells singing down to her from atop the hill. Looking behind her, she saw a dark man helming the ship, sparks of fire around his head. To her left

*she saw herself, walking on the sea alongside her ship, with a
fox running frantic circles about her. Feeling a sense of shocking
familiarity, Riley moved closer to speak to her doppelgänger. Sensing
Riley's movement, the doppelgänger stopped – and the world
stopped with her. She turned at looked at Riley, and Riley was
filled with dread. The doppelgänger's skull was opened above the
eyebrows; brain exposed, electric currents crawling over its surface.
Her eyes were fixed as if upon a distant horror, a rictus grin etched
onto her face. She mouthed* eímai to méllon. *Below her, under the
clear Aegean water, darkness snaked through the depths towards
the gleaming city on the hill.*

*The fox leapt onto the deck near Riley, autumn fur standing in
stark contrast to the pitched wood.*

Kill that thing – kill it.

*The sea went to turmoil, and the stranger began to tremble as
if in anticipation of what was to come. A great roaring wind swept
over the sea. Ships in the distance were scattered, masts tipping
under the wind like trees flattening in a storm. Ocean waves dashed
ships against rocks along the shoreline, loud crashes of wood and
metal drowning out the screams of the passengers. Alarms rang in
the distance as panic gripped the world. Riley felt a presence behind
her, spun and struck at emptiness, knowing that her hand would
collide with metal.* First Officer Riley Carter jolted awake roughly,
her left hand bleeding after smashing against the inside wall of her
cryotank.

What the hell.

Riley extracted herself, surrounded by eerie silence. No other
crew present, and all of the cryotanks were empty. She made her
way in darkness, from the crew quarters to the *Shé Chengzai's*
centrally located control room. Walls that should have housed
bioluminescent algae stood dark, and the systems housed within
the walls lay silent. Riley's optics were at maximum gain, and green
sparks danced through her vision as she moved.

She arrived at the command centre, her optics rapidly adjusting
to light coming from the room. She heard a man speaking, picked
up the flattened tones and recognized it as a recording.

Captain Lau was at his station, seemingly oblivious to the world
as he intently watched a holographic message from Dr Dubhghall.
Riley connected to the nearest station, still watching the Captain,
and began accessing the ships systems. *Gods.*

Most of the ships systems had failed or were failing. The QG system and communications were operational, but nearly everything else was listed in red or had gone completely dark. Power was out to all cryotanks. Life support had substantially failed – there were a few hours of clean air left, and nothing else.

There was a whisper in her ear. *Your crew is dead.*

Panic gripped Riley and she let out a soft moan. Lau stiffened and turned towards her. "Oh Riley! I'm so glad you joined us!" He strode to her side, dark circles around his eyes.

"What happened Lau?" It was statement as much as it was a question.

"I told you. We are going to found a brave new world for humanity."

"Where is the crew?"

"You know that we aren't human. You made sure to point it out every chance you had. I agree with you, you know. So if we're to build a new kingdom for humanity, we must make sure that only humanity exists on this world. So I've cleared the way."

While he spoke, Riley frantically raced through the ships data until she found what she wanted; it wasn't a single cycle later, the *Shé Chengzai* was entering terminal orbit around Wolf 1061c as they stood there.

Another whisper. *Kill that thing – kill it.*

Without warning she struck Lau in the throat. He gasped, eyes wide in shock and pain. Turning, she ran, headed for the sole atmospheric craft. Running through darkness she could hear a building roar coming from the outer walls as the thin atmosphere of the planet began to caress the skin of the *Shé Chengzai*.

She arrived just as thrust gave way to freefall; up and down became meaningless. *No time to suit up.* Strapping herself in, she raced through the startup procedures, ignoring a cacophony of alarms. The atmospheric roar had become deafening. *Eject the pod.* Riley gave the command. The small craft tore a gash through the side of the ship as it leapt away. The *Shé Chengzai* turned over, fatally wounded, and fell towards hungry rock below amidst shrieks of twisting metal. Ribbons of orange fire licked out at Riley's craft as she punched through violet atmosphere. Overhead, a pale green moon limned the glass and metal angles of her craft as it tumbled through the atmosphere. The spin of the craft forced blood to her head, turning her vision red. Sparks floated about the cabin and dancing flame leapt to her hair. As the craft nosed down, Riley saw the pastel colours give way to deepest blue, and then all colour retreated from her world as the advancing darkness took her.

SALVATION
DAVE BRADLEY

//Impact +1 Minute//

At first the light was so piercing and pervasive that it was like witnessing a nuclear airblast. Only the absence of heat told Peter otherwise.

And the fact that he was still alive.

His skin tingled but the pins and needles soon faded.

"Welcome, friend. You're safe. You're all safe."

He squinted and the universe dimmed and deepened into focus. Sight, smell, touch, sound, even the taste of the air on his panting tongue. It was beautiful, almost euphoric, like every summer's day at once.

Grass grew around, the intense green of a ripe apple. Sturdy trees rustled in air redolent of honeysuckle and jasmine.

In front of him stood a tall, thin and silver-skinned figure, with the biggest eyes Peter had ever seen. As he swayed, trying to remember how to balance, the creature unfurled a pair of glittering wings. They resembled a multitude of slender golden threads, little blue sparks pulsing up and around them to the tip and back.

A slender hand reached out to him.

"Is this heaven?" Peter asked.

"No, friend," said the figure, with what might have been a laugh. "Not quite."

//Impact -72 Hours//

The tumbling rock cast a shadow over everything.

Peter was far from the colony, alone in the cramped rocket capsule, and The Bastard had been visible in the soot-black sky the whole time. Points of light glinted from it where ineffectual probes had landed over the last few weeks. Strapped in his capsule, he'd been fired from the Outer Belt asteroid outpost in a direction no human had been in his lifetime. They'd dispatched signals and received replies. Those altered folk on the edge of space... they knew he was coming.

Peter was the new ambassador from Earth's mining colonies to the One Transhuman Polity. He gnawed on a fingernail and it hurt. Most Belters had cured themselves of the nervous habit years back. In a zero-G environment, chewed bits of human debris are unpleasant at best. But here, on the threshold of the most important meeting of his life, he indulged himself.

Hours passed.

He arrived with no fanfare. Unseen hands tugged the capsule into a huge unlit bay. Peter stepped out, his feet heavy like a navy captain landing in a foreign harbour, unsure of the rules and certain he'd broken a few already. The chamber was as high as a cathedral, with laser-cut walls of rock. There was space in here for a score of craft like his own, but his was alone.

The One Transhuman Polity lived, if you could call it living, inside an asteroid. Perhaps one like The Bastard itself. But this one had a controlled trajectory, and patrolled a region of space claimed by the outsiders as their own.

There were many thousands of beings believed to exist in the Polity, but since Earth had severed ties nobody knew. The UN had outlawed AI, human modification, cybernetic experimentation and other technologies that the Polity embraced. So they'd departed, in their words, 'to grow and explore.' The humans left behind on Earth and its inner colonies feared them, although they wouldn't admit it. The two peoples, with such opposing ideologies, had not communicated in one hundred years.

But Peter's people needed their help.

There was no welcoming party. No official delegation, no diplomatic reception. But as Peter loosened his helmet, someone appeared in the centre of the cavern, as if entering through a door Peter could not see.

A creature, an outsider. It was short, the height of an adolescent, and smooth, as though made of plastic. A bipedal humanoid in shape but not male or female in the way Peter's people understood. The worst kind of person, the Ambassador's teachers had always told him. An embodiment of rejected humanity, of hubris and corruption. Not like us. On instinct he both hated and feared whatever stood before him, its robotic blandness an affront to some primal part of his psyche. It was the chill of facing a chamber of horrors waxwork. This herald looked as out of place beneath the vaulted stone as a child's doll would look in the nave of Westminster Abbey.

"Hello! Welcome, friend, welcome," said the Polity's androgyne messenger. Peter blinked and raised his eyebrows. The voice was soft, warm even, but confident too, a soul not as afraid of this first encounter as Peter. If this was a robot, it didn't speak like one.

Before the Ambassador could answer, the herald continued: "I am Interface Three." It extended a slender hand, on which sat a pill. "I'm sorry, but to begin negotiations with the One Transhuman Polity, you must swallow this."

"What is it?" Peter frowned then shrugged. Yes, those were the first human words spoken to the representative of a long-lost culture. He picked up the pill. His fingertips just brushed his host's palm, which was as cold as the room. The pill was the size of a button from a duffle coat, and translucent. It writhed inside with a score of what looked like miniature spiders, scrabbling over each other. The pill seemed alive.

"Don't be alarmed, friend. It's a translation tool, nothing else. It's essential." The herald's voice was calm and its smooth face attempted an apologetic smile. "Those are little machines we've made for you - if that makes it any easier to swallow."

It didn't, but Peter placed the pill on his tongue and gulped at once, so he didn't have to suffer it bursting and scuttling in his mouth.

A few seconds after it hit his stomach, the universe exploded with luminescence. Information swamped him, assaulted his thoughts, caressed them. He passed out, and unseen arms caught him.

//Impact -68 Hours//

He saw what they saw. Data everywhere, lights on every surface, neon detail in the rock. There were presences around him, a variety of beings. Larger and smaller and brighter than humans. Folk with skin of quartz and limbs stretching as far as their imagination allowed. All shared silently; conversation at the speed of electricity. There was no distinction between the real and the virtual.

He was afraid, but they were kind. He asked for their help, without words, because memory and vocabulary were different here. Meaning was everywhere, like oxygen had been everywhere on Earth. They breathed awareness instead of air. He was attached to them and they could see through him.

"You're here to discuss the asteroid cluster B7-482 and the recent orbital anomaly," they said, or all seemed to know and think at the same time.

Peter blinked at the brightness of his new vision. He saw deeper and sharper. The world around him grew, enhanced by dots and lines and blinking lights inside his brain. He swallowed and said, or dreamed he said: "Us Belters call the mineral-heavy bodies nearest our colony, The Family. Our mining efforts knocked one of them out of the field and onto-"

"A collision course with your outpost. We predicted it and modelled such a collision before you even began probing the region."

"We call the rogue asteroid The Bastard. It'll impact in under three days."

"Sad that it takes such a potential catastrophe to overcome the prejudice that has separated our peoples for generations."

"But you can help?"

"We can and we will. With pleasure."

Peter's people distrusted these outsiders, had done for generations. But now, plugged in to them, he knew warmth and hope. "You can stop the collision."

A pause in the data. Then a rush that was part emotion, part statistics. "No, friend. But we have prepared for your evacuation."

//Impact -2 Hours//

Had any on Earth's farthest colony stopped fighting for places on the evacuation capsules and looked out of their viewing ports, they would have seen two objects in the sky. One dark and one bright.

The shadowy shape falling towards them from the west was The Bastard. The bright shape was a ship of the One Transhuman Polity.

It was round and vast at its core and surrounded by nanoprobes that shone amber, like fireflies, and made the vessel resemble a large Chinese lantern drifting on the breeze. Streamers of silver trailed behind it, reaching out like the prehensile tails of rats. It was a mechanical swarm tunnelling through space. As the craft neared the colony, the nanoprobes and inquisitor filaments swarmed towards the human structures.

Peter stood on what he'd taken to calling the deck of the Transhuman ship, although there were no controls or windows. Everything was virtual, projected into his consciousness and appearing around him, an enhanced reality he shared with his new allies.

"When will the evacuation begin?" he asked, beaming his thoughts to the other entities. "How will we get them all up here?"

His mind's eye looked outside and below the craft, following the fibres as they punched into the colony shields. They reached down and sought the human refugees.

As proximity data showed The Bastard's unstoppable trajectory towards the colony, Peter realised that this was no physical evacuation. He opened his mouth to shout something, a natural instinct in the unnatural silence.

The swallowed spider machines shut him off from existence, along with all of his kind. And joyfully, kindly, relentlessly, the Polity database gathered their souls. The upload began.

//Impact +1 Minute//

At first the light was so piercing and pervasive that it was like witnessing a nuclear airblast. Then the universe dimmed into focus: it was almost euphoric.

In front of Peter stood a figure, tall and thin and silver-skinned, with the biggest eyes he'd ever seen. The herald unfurled a pair of wings made of slender golden threads. Little blue electrical pulses played up and down them. A slender hand reached out. Peter took it and it steadied him. Around them the too-green grass flickered like bad static for a moment.

There were people nearby, familiar faces, blinking into existence.

"Welcome, friend. You're safe. You're all safe."

"Is this heaven?" Peter asked.

"No, friend," said Interface Three's virtual avatar, smiling. "Not quite. It's better than that. You're with us now."

A SIGNAL IN THE DARK

PETER SUTTON.

R hea planted her feet wide and slammed the beacon into the regolith. The beacon's simple AI kicked in as the probe burrowed its way into the planetoid and the beacon's flashing red light became a baleful lighthouse to the void; broadcasting Jianxi's claim to the minerals and providing a homing beacon to the mother mining ship, the Aphra.

She recited the company protocol without reference to the little plastic card all scout ships were given. "I claim this solar body in the name of the Jianxi mining corporation in accordance with the laws set under directive 22a. I formally renounce any claim over this land in return for the usual finder's fee."

It was a stupid and pointless piece of bureaucracy but kept claim disputes to a minimum.

Most of the Trans-Neptune Orbit bodies had been found, labelled, claimed and plundered but scouts like her still occasionally came across ones, like this, that neither of the big mining companies had on their records.

Back onboard she heated some slop in a cup. She took the steaming mug and plopped into the drive seat, As she spooned the 'tasty' nutrimeat into her mouth she scanned the nearest TNO's. The Oort was a million miles from Titan (well thousands of AU's anyway) – arse end of the Solar System. As expected nothing was happening. She swirled the slop around her mouth, it was bland but EVA's always made her hungry, it was Pavlovian.

***

"Safie put the ball away!" Always the child made noise.

"Safie are you listening to me?"

Rhea sighed and clambered out of bed, the sound of the ball bouncing against the hull repetitive and annoying. It almost sounded electronic, the squeak it made against the metal. The ship hummed in sleep and Rhea didn't want to wake too much. Safie playing with a ball would do it though.

"Safie! You know I have to go to work in the morning."

She cursed as she stood on some piece of a toy awaiting her like a caltrop.

"Safie! You stop this instant! If you haven't stopped by the time I get to your bedroom I'll--" The sound of the ball stopped and Rhea sighed again. She pushed the door open onto her child's dark room.

Safie was in the corner, head bowed, long blonde hair like a waterfall over her legs. Her tiny hand clutching a red ball.

"Safie, you should be in bed, come on now." Rhea put on her stern voice and climbed on the bed, fluffed a pillow and then patted it. "It's time to sleep."

"No."

"Safie, don't answer back, it's time to sleep, it's time little girls like you were in bed."

"No." The child shook her head violently, threw the ball against the wall and then caught it.

"Safie, I--"

Safie threw the ball again but this time mistimed the catch. As the ball bounced over to the bed she turned to watch and Rhea's breath caught in her throat.

The girl's deep, black eyes bored into her, staring from a grey, rotting face set in a rictus grin.

"I don't need to sleep Momma. I'm dead, remember?"

Rhea sat up clutching her cold, clammy chest, heart stuttering. She clapped the light on and waited for her breathing to calm. Safie had been dead for five years, she usually only dreamt about her when very anxious.

The dreams where Safie was alive were worse, then she awoke feeling happy, but reality asserted itself with a crash. The nightmares were easier to bear. At least that's what she told herself.

It had been a stupid accident that had taken her little girl away. The headmaster of the Vale school had been skimping on maintenance in order to shave extra profit from the obscene amounts he charged the parents. There'd been a seal failure, a slow outgassing, faulty emergency procedures, faulty doors. In all, twelve children had died.

"I see you're already awake," the AI chirped, "you have a message."

Distress signal coming from Orcus please investigate, she read.

Distress signal?

"Ship, do we have a claim on Orcus?"

"No, that's one of Vale's."

"Fucking Mudders!" Rhea spat. "Can we ignore it?"

"Rules are rules." A phrase the AI had used a few times before with her.

"Fuck." She supposed it made sense. If she was in trouble she'd accept help from anyone, including Mudders, but she wouldn't like it.

"Okay, set a course." She finished her slop glumly and tapped out a reply. Now to have a rubdown and change out of the suit. Dreaming of Safie reminded her of Titan and The Zone. Full of Vale's bigwig brats. That's why she'd taken a job with Jianxi. Working for the competition was a small revenge every day.

When she got back to the console she was surprised to see a request for a two-way comm. She thumbed the panel to open the link.

"Rhea, what a pleasure it is to see you up and dressed!" The blond face of Stevenson filled the screen, his clean white teeth set in a stupid grin.

"You're never going to let me forget that are you?" she groaned.

"Aww, I thought your bed head was cute."

Once, when she was relatively new to the scout business she'd thought a request for a two-way comm was an emergency and had answered despite just waking up. Naked. Not that he'd seen anything, but it was obvious that she'd been unclothed, and of course he'd said something and she'd blushed.

She wasn't much of a blusher any more though.

"What's up?" she asked.

Stevenson sighed and, rubbing his beard, switched to business. "That distress call you're on your way to?"

"The Mudder one?"

Stevenson winced. "The Vale one, yes. Well it's only the son of the big boss. That's got the brass's knickers in a twist."

"Baxter's precious boy, out here?"

"Seems so. So act delicately and put on your Sunday best spacesuit. And for God's sake don't call him a Mudder to his face!" Stevenson itched his ear, sure sign that there was something else. It was one of the tells she used to fleece him at cards when she was aboard the mining ship.

"What else?" she asked with a sigh.

"Well... "

"Yeah, spit it out man!"

"Joby answered the call too."

"And what? You think that just because we split and I broke his jaw for cheating on me, we won't be able to be professional?" Wait till she saw that little shit, there was definitely unfinished business there.

The reason she'd been in the Zone in the first place was because of Joby. He'd insisted that their little girl go to the best school on Titan. Together they could just about afford the fees, but if your child's education wasn't important what was?

When Safie died they split. Badly.

"Just, you know, try not to kill him until after the job is done." Stevenson only knew some of the story, Joby had been mostly absent even when they were together. Safie's death had been the end though. She'd left an uncomfortable pause.

142

"I'll try."

After signing off she thought she should thank Stevenson for the heads-up. When she got back she'd buy him a drink.

"Ship, what's our ETA?"

"Four hours, seven minutes and twenty three seconds."

"Right, I'm going to rest my eyes, tell me when we're thirty minutes away."

Of course after being reminded of Joby she dreamed of Titan. Of their apartment, owned, like everything in the Zone, by the mining corp. All the facts from that horrible day, a day she couldn't forget no matter how she'd tried to blot it, came rushing back.

Of course the man responsible had got off on some technicality. Although he'd committed suicide, couldn't live with twelve dead kids on his conscience. She dreamt again of the vidcast of the news of his death. The awful sinking feeling as she realised he'd escaped.

***

The binary of Orcus and Vanth filled the screen and a list of facts scrolled down the right hand side. Rhea could see the mining ship squatting on the planet like a giant leech. The distress signal was just the standard CQD, no other signal or explanation.

Rhea rubbed her eyes then ran her fingers through her stubbly hair. God damn Joby and God damn all fucking Mudders. She took a long slow inhale, held it then blew it out explosively. Time to go to work.

"Ship, can you zoom in on the mining ship at all?"

The image on the screen zoomed in. Everything looked normal. But she could only see one side of the ship, the other being in deep shadow.

"I have failed to handshake with the Vale ship," the AI informed her.

"Neither of them?" Rhea asked, searching the image for a transporter.

"There is only the mining ship there," the AI responded.

Curious.

"Check Vanth?"

"I have done. There are no other ships here."

No other ships. Perhaps her ex, Joby had been and gone and never bothered to tell her? But he'd have told the Aphra surely?

"Ship, can you do a search for nearby scouts?" Rhea rubbed sleep out of her eyes and slurped the last of her coffee. Time to suit up.

"Scanning."

As the ship approached the landing pad the AI informed her that there were no other scouts in range of her sensors.

Curiouser and curiouser.

Rhea broke out the regulation sidearm and strapped it to her leg. "What do you think this is? High Noon at the Mudder corral?" she murmured to herself. She must be nervous, she only talked to herself when she was nervous.

She asked the ship to ping a message to the Aphra to say she'd landed.

***

Little puffs of red dust followed her giant steps across the planetoid. It was rich in iron, which was why she assumed the mining ship was here. She wondered where the Mudder mothership was. And why it hadn't sent anyone to come and rescue the son of the boss.

The airlock was wide open. Both doors, complete decompression. If Baxter wasn't in a suit this was going to be a very short rescue mission. The power was off, on emergency lights only, the CQD on a loop.

She headed to the control room. She hated Vale ships, so cramped. Their tiny Mudder bodies needed less room than her people. All that gravity crushing them into dwarfs.

She surveyed the wreckage a meteor had strewn across what was left of the control room. Anyone on the ship, and she'd seen no sign of life as yet, would have had seconds to suit up after an explosive decompression. At least there'd been no fire, no Oxygen to burn.

This ship was going nowhere. The engines were still sound, but the brain of the ship was dead. So where was Baxter? Did he have Oxygen? The ship failed to generate an atmosphere.

She did a thorough search. No-one. She found a vid-cube which, from a quick glance, was Baxter sending a message to someone called Madeleine. She pocketed it and made her way to the airlock.

"Ship?"

Rhea listened to her own breathing and frowned. "Ship?"

No answer.

As she thumbed the door release she spotted a puff of gas coming from her own ship. A hull breach?

She bounced across to her ship as fast as she could. Beneath it lay a jumble of equipment. She frowned. What had he done? "Ship?"

Inside it was worse. The command centre was dark. The AI, dead. The ship was grounded. That fucking Mudder must have been hiding somewhere and took the opportunity to destroy her ship whilst she was searching for him. To rescue him. She turned the air blue. She took a calming breath. She could still fly without the AI, if nothing else important was broken.

Outside her heart sank to see vital components smashed beyond repair. She glanced across to the mining ship. There could be parts there she could possibly scavenge and jury rig. She was dead in a few hours if she couldn't get the oxygen generator working.

A shadow passed above her and she glanced up to see another scout ship in low orbit. Joby. So maybe she didn't need to scavenge anything.

"Hey Joby, can you hear me?"

"Yes I can hear you." Joby sounded flat, angry?

"Well get your arse down here, that fucking Mudder has wrecked my ship!" She fingered her gun, scanning the planetoid for movement. The dark blotting out of stars that was Vanth stole across the landscape, creeping ever closer.

"No, Rhea, he didn't."

"What are you talking about? He's killed the AI and wrecked the engines, I'm dead in the water here." She continued to scan her surroundings. There were lots of hiding places.

"It wasn't him, Rhea."

That was the annoying thing about Joby. She'd been attracted to his taciturnity, assuming, naively, that still waters ran deep. However in Joby's case it was all shallows.

"Well there's no-one else here to do it… " Apart from Joby that is. But he wouldn't, would he?

"The Aphra was very sad to hear about your accident, Rhea." He sounded tired rather than angry. "I'm sure that the reward that Baxter senior is offering for the return of his boy will assuage my obvious grief at your predicament."

"You fucker."

"That's what I like about you Rhea, always so ladylike."

"I'll kill you!" She started bounding towards the mining ship. That fucking Mudder offering a reward? That was just so typical of those grasping planet-crawlers, everything was about money. Fuck Baxter and fuck his son.

"You tried that already, remember? I was sucking my meals through a straw for weeks. I swore that I'd pay you back for that. Getting a reward to do so is going to be so sweet."

"Be a man. Come and kill me. Because if you leave me here I *will* escape and will track you down and *will* kill you." She reached the mining ship and yomped to the engines.

"With Junior here unconscious and no-one else going to come rescue you, my version of events will be the truth. By the time anyone comes to collect the scrap you'll be long forgotten." The orbiting scout ship's rockets fired and the ship moved off. "So long Rhea, and good riddance."

She didn't waste her breath to reply.

Twenty minutes later she knew she was fucked. The Vale engine design was vastly different from hers. If she'd had specialist tools, and a lot of time, she could potentially jig something together. If her AI was sound she could possibly have combined it with the mining ship somehow. Think Rhea, think.

She bounced back to her ship, perhaps she could get the communicator working? An honest appraisal of the mess Joby had left the instrument panel in told her otherwise.

She had possibly twelve hours of oxygen, neither ship would generate an atmosphere, however the mining ship's generator was fine although the hull was breached catastrophically. There was nothing wrong with her hull. Since she couldn't think of how to get off-planet, how to keep herself alive for longer than twelve hours?

The mining ship had some cutting tools and she had a small maintenance kit aboard her scout. Four hours of cutting, lumping equipment across the surface and soldering later and she had an oxygen generator. OK so it might not have been working at maximum efficiency but it was going to keep her alive and give her a lot more than twelve hours.

Now to the more intractable problem. Over hot food and drink, thank the stars Joby hadn't sabotaged the micro-kitchen, she puzzled it out. She had a very real problem – people thought that Baxter was saved, so would ignore the CQD, and that she was dead, so not a priority to retrieve her body. She had no next of kin, her folks back on Titan had died years ago, she was split from Joby, and Safie was gone. Stevenson would raise a hip flask to her memory and that was about it. Getting mixed up in Mudder business had fucked her yet again. First Safie, now this.

She was dead on her feet, she had to sleep on her problem, but she needed to fuel her body too, lots of physical exertion needed lots of calories, needed lots of slop.

***

She was back on Titan, it played in her dreams over and over. The graveyard. She ran her hand over the gravestone, the span of years accorded to her daughter pathetically small, and wiped a tear away. She whispered a prayer, not believing a word of it. He'll be punished, her mouth said, her eyes hard, determined not to cry.

She turned and there was another grave. The Mudder that had killed her daughter. His lifespan many multiples of hers. Even if he'd taken his own life. He didn't deserve to be in a grave, didn't deserve to be remembered with anything but contempt. She found she had a beacon in her hand and rammed it into the grave. It's flashing red light a warning and a message. This is not for you Mudders. Jianxi come and strip this place.

The red flashing light.

***

As she awoke she remembered the red flashing light. Of course, the beacons, She had about twenty of them. She couldn't reprogram them but she could put them in an aesthetically pleasing SOS shape for when the Aphra came over the horizon; the multitude of homing signals would definitely grab the its attention.

She could hardly get the suit on fast enough. Why hadn't she thought of it before? Exhausted from lugging all that equipment, stressed and angry too.

Later, as she stood back and admired her giant blinking SOS, she allowed herself to fantasise about catching up with Joby. She hoped that Stevenson, or one of the other officers, was, even now, trying to contact her. When they couldn't, they'd know her comms were out and send someone.

The signal would take a while to get through, she could add a few more calories with breakfast. As ever the EVA had left her feeling hungry. She was sure she'd soon be burning them off.

Four hours later and no sign of a rescue ship. OK the Aphra had been days away but there must be another scout out here? She wasn't used to idleness, and it gave her too much time to think, about everything. So she decided to see what else was salvageable from the Mudder ship. She spent a few hours collecting a pile of things that could be re-used.

Later, back on her own ship, she thought she was too wound up for sleep, but her eyes sagged closed anyway. She hoped she wouldn't dream again.

***

A bright flash woke her and as she stumbled to the porthole she slapped her hand to her hip to feel the reassuring weight of the gun. If Joby had come back she was going to shoot the bastard.

A ship, a sleek, but obviously Mudder, ship, descended on a pillar of smoke from out of the heavens. She was ready to leave at a moment's notice so she grabbed her helmet and made her way to the airlock.

She stood outside her ship and watched the two squat figures bound over. Both held firearms. She frowned at that and her hand hovered near her own gun.

"Drop the weapon and put your hands up!" a voice, low, guttural, Earth-accented, ordered.

She shrugged, took her gun from its holster and threw it to one side.

"Now, get on your knees," the voice ordered.

"I'm not *a* danger. I'm *in* danger!" she protested.

"Do it! Now!" The two figures gestured with their guns. She reluctantly complied. One of them covered her, the other gambolled over, moved behind her and grabbed her hands and tied them behind her back with what felt like cable ties.

"Hey!" she protested, but the figure behind her bundled her to the floor.

"Secure!" A woman's voice.

"Now you'll see what you get for attacking Vale employees and destroying company property," the first, male, said.

"I didn't do—"

"Quiet!"

Rhea struggled and swore and ranted but they bundled her securely and ignored her shouted imprecations so that she eventually fell silent.

The two Mudders frogmarched her to their ship. She wasn't allowed to grab any personal items. The woman had done a cursory search. Rhea got no reply when she'd asked them what they were looking for.

She was shoved into a hastily emptied cargo space, barely enough room to sit, and the door locked. The ship took off, Rhea was jostled and bruised as she wasn't strapped down. Then the artificial gravity kicked in and it pulled at her like none she'd ever felt before. It must have matched Earth's gravity. She had trouble breathing and she ached as the G's sucked at her.

The woman, stout, like all Mudders, burst into the room and wrestled Rhea's helmet off.

"Let's see what a would-be murderess looks like!"

As the helmet came off Rhea took a long breath and closed her eyes. Opening them again she stared into a snarling face.

"Murderess?"

"Yes you lanky bastard, a murderess." The woman sat back on her haunches. Rhea was prone, she'd not managed to get up after launch.

"I'm no murderess, nor attempted one either."

"So why did you attack Baxter and try and prevent your fellow Giraffe from rescuing him then?" the woman grunted and stood, not waiting for an answer.

Giraffe? That's what the Mudders called people from the outer planets. Just because they were naturally taller having grown in a lower gravity. What had Joby told them?

"Whatever Joby said is a lie!" she tried.

"Tell it to the judge," the woman threw back before closing the door.

No matter how she looked at it this was bad. But at least she was no longer on Orcus, right?

***

After a few hours they fed her and took the cable ties off. As she tried to rub some life back into her hands she tried to get some sense out of them. From what the man said she assumed that Joby had spun a tale of her and Baxter fighting over mining rights, her attacking Baxter and Joby riding to the rescue. The nerve of the man!

She put her side to them. They didn't buy it. But she asked that they contact Stevenson on the Aphra who'd back up at least part of her story. That she'd responded to the distress signal.

After they were gone she tried to make herself comfortable and something sharp jabbed her in the hip. The vid-cube! The woman hadn't taken it away.

She took it out and pressed play. Maybe Baxter explained why he'd called for help. If her captors didn't trust her maybe they'd trust him? She placed the cube on the floor as the features of Baxter, a typical Mudder, short, muscular, thick featured, sprang into view. He was helmetless, not the best sign, he looked tired; perhaps this was before the accident?

"Hey Madeleine. Hey you. It's daddy. I had to go far away, remember? Well look."

Baxter grabbed the camera and panned it around the ship. Rhea recognised the one she'd been scavenging from but in pristine condition. He pointed the camera out of the window and the familiar binary of Orcus and Vanth could be seen as the ship approached them.

"Grandpa and daddy had an argument honey. That's why daddy had to go. Had to prove to grandpa that daddy could do a good job. That he could provide for his daughter"

The camera swung back to point at Baxter again.

"That's why daddy is in space. I'll be back real soon, just as soon as I've collected a ton of ore. Love you and miss you."

There was a fade.

The vid clicked on to a scene of utter chaos. A helmeted Baxter sat in front of a kaleidoscope of small flying debris, the command centre far in the background a maelstrom as the atmosphere disappeared.

"Maddy, be good for your mother. I love you! It might take me a bit longer to come home."

Baxter looked off-screen as there was a loud noise, like a tree cracking in the wind. Something fast swiped him away from the screen, then the screen itself tumbled, went black.

Rhea had her hand to her mouth. Baxter knew that everything was going to shit and his first thought was to contact his daughter. She had been gritting her teeth when she first started watching. What advantage could she get with the vid? How could she use it to get one over on those people? But now? She sat stunned.

Baxter was just a father who loved his daughter and was trying to do what was best for her. To show her that he wasn't a good for nothing. Her cheeks blazed yet also felt wet. He was just like her. She wondered when she'd started thinking that they were all evil, all culpable, and realised that Joby's casual bigotry had seeped into her soul at some point and put down roots after Safie's death. Caused by a Mudder. The very word one of Joby's...

She banged on the door. Her captors, no longer just Mudders but other folk, needed to see this. It exonerated her, it showed that Baxter was injured in the accident.

The woman was the one that came, her face full of suspicion.

"Here, watch this." Rhea thumbed play and handed it to the woman who reluctantly turned her eyes to the video. When it finished the woman didn't say anything, she just closed the door and took the vid-cube with her.

***

Rhea waited for her boarding call. The transporter that would return her to Titan was predictably delayed. The Vale base on Neso was where the scout ship that had picked her up on Orcus had deposited her. They'd consulted with Vale head office, as well as the Aphra, and by general consensus she was exonerated and freed. No apology.

She'd had to pay for transport herself. The Aphra would return to Titan in a few months and she could sign back on if she wanted to. Joby had brought Baxter here to Neso and then left again, destination unknown. Guilt assuaged by the payout he'd received from Baxter senior.

Her ship was lost, she'd get a fraction of its cost through insurance but she was still alive at least. There was some activity at the boarding desk, it wouldn't be long now. She sighed and returned to her book but looked up as a shadow fell across it.

"Hello." Baxter junior seemed younger in person than he had on the vid.

She put the book down and stood, found herself shaking his out-thrust hand.

"Mr Baxter, this is unexpected."

"Rhea, isn't it? Can I call you Rhea?" he smiled, his seeming self-assurance belied by the searching quality of his eyes.

"Sure," she was at a loss. What did he want?

"I thought I'd come and thank you for returning the vid-cube. And for coming to save my life, even if that didn't go to plan."

"You're welcome. How's your daughter?"

Baxter smiled genuinely this time. "Very happy her daddy is home and not likely to run off back into space alone any time soon. She's looking forward to getting me home."

Rhea smiled in return. The first boarding call was given, people who needed assistance, people with children, gold card members etc. "Good, good, I'm glad. It was nice of you to come and see me off," she said grabbing her bag ready to join the economy queue.

"I just thought I should come and tell you that the man who brought me here, Joby, he was heading to Mars. He had some plan to spend his money on a little unit there and stop tramping across the Kuiper belt and Oort cloud." Baxter offered his hand again.

As she shook it Rhea asked, "why tell me?"

"I've read up on you. I'm sorry about your daughter. You didn't deserve what that man did to you. His treatment of me was entirely motivated by greed. I grow tired of people who only ever seek to take advantage of me." He smiled again as they shook hands. "You'd best get on, wouldn't want to miss your flight. It was good meeting you."

"Nice to meet you too," she said automatically. He gave her one last grin then strode off as she turned and joined the shuffling line on its way to the transporter.

Mars! It made sense she supposed. It had mostly Earth colonies but there were plenty of people from the outer planets that had made their home there too. It was still sparsely populated, the gravity wasn't as crushing as Earth, and it was a big planet to get lost on. They'd even talked about it, gathering enough money to retire to Mars and get a little place. Once she settled in her seat she'd see how much a ticket to Mars would cost.

***

Rhea visualised Joby waking from the deep dark dream the drugs she'd slipped into his food unit would have put him in. He wouldn't be sure what had woken him, some noise? As she thought about him fumbling in the dark she wondered if he'd realise it wasn't a sound, it was lack of noise. The lights wouldn't switch on. The entire compound would be dark. There'd still be a hiss from the atmospherics but all the other usual machinery noises would be ominously silent. She grinned and checked her chronometer, he'd slumber for hours after he consumed the doctored slop. The hardest part was waiting, motionless, hidden behind the panels, for him to stumble to bed. Sabotaging his pod was child's play.

She pictured him rushing in panic to the suits, where he'd find them slashed and useless, all but one. That's when he'd find her note.

Joby

I did promise that I'd kill you but I've had a bit of a change of heart. So I'm going to give you the same chance you gave me. Give or take.

I've disabled all but the life support. You have no transport. No communications and no portable oxygen.

Unlike what you did to me, one of your neighbours could probably wander past and rescue you. You have been making friends haven't you? You've not just been hiding out?

Unlike you I don't have a big payout to moderate my guilt.

I'll be going back to Titan to visit our daughter's grave.

I consider us to be even. Don't make the mistake of escalating this.

Rhea.

His nearest neighbour was around sixty km away. She hoped the darkness outside of Joby's window would seem very lonely.

***

As Rhea's shuttle took off she relaxed back in her seat and took out a photograph of her daughter. Safie was wearing a green party dress, holding a fairy wand and grinning without a care in the world. It had been taken on her birthday, she hadn't seen another one. Rhea smiled sadly and whispered, "I'm coming home Safie. No more running away."

FAST LOVE DIE

DAVID J RODGER

The twin beams of the Xenon headlamps shredded the darkness but the forest held onto the shadows. Trent Faber pushed the Sarotik's speed towards the top line; compression springs soaked up most of the shocks but the whole frame was leaping around the road like a bitch faking an orgasm.

Trent wasn't superstitious. He didn't believe in magic. But this place always gave him the damned heebs. Ever since he'd been a kid, growing up in Bolinas resenting the rich pricks who drifted up from San Francisco like tourists. He'd been stealing their cars since he'd been old enough to reach the pedals. And this place, the Wapasha Ridge, always seemed to be the place he wound up at the end of a hard ride.

Now he was out here to kill a man.

It felt like destiny had been hinting at him all this time: this place means something. It holds significance in your life!

And these ancient trees were a witness. Of what he would do to do to help the girl he loved. A girl called Krysta Stine.

Nahuel Rock was where the meet had been planned. Site of many myths and legends – massacres by white people and Indians alike. Stories of ghosts and vengeful spirits that stalked the lonely hours when the fog tended to roll in from the coast.

The Sheriff's Office had found plenty of bodies out here – torn apart. Some were the result of wolves. Some were big cats. Some were the Wayra Skulls who practiced blood sacrifice at places along the ridge – when they weren't tearing up the small towns on Hopper Trikes or cooking up low-grade Pentathene IV in filthy underground chem-labs. Trent knew the scene. Crime and Law. Like this road, they were woven into the tapestry of his life.

One more dead body wasn't going to turn too many heads.

Strange how life had a way of playing with synchronicity. Him thinking that at that very moment...

It was the curve before the long straight leading down to Nahuel Rock and the nearby shoreline. He came out of the apex of the bend accelerating hard, looking to punch out as much speed from the monster as he could along the line. As the headlights raked the trees, sweeping back to point down the barrel of the road, a guy appeared – like a ghost. Facing away, the figure seemed familiar but there wasn't any time to react let alone try to reason why. The figure barely began to twist around, as if in shock, before the impact. Trent saw the man's body flung up, twisting away like a rag doll and out of sight in the dark. His foot was already slamming the brakes, too late. Fought the control paddle as the rear-wheels tried to swing the car around.

He stopped at a slant across the road. Heart-pounding, not quite believing what had just happened. Dizzy on adrenaline, he slapped the Nanomech controls and the transparent panel on the driver's side melted away bringing in the smell of high-octane biofuel. Then came the smell of the forest, a pungent heady aroma that was unlike anywhere else on Earth. He stared through the opening and listened. Nothing but the sounds of night. Nothing moved. Was the guy still alive? Badly injured? Trent had a moment of moral debate. He bit down on his lip as his thoughts focused around the gun lying on the passenger-side seat. He didn't have time for this. The Sarotik wasn't his. He didn't need to worry about the damage or anybody tracing another dead body back to him. Decision made, Trent gunned the accelerator and held on as the wheels kicked up a spray of dirt before gripping the weathered road and propelling him forward.

***

Farouk Abdl Musa had a face like somebody had tried to push him violently back into the womb at birth. A broad nose that was so flat against his skull it looked squashed; dark, mean eyes and a tall narrow forehead that marked out his Somali ancestry. He'd probably spent his entire life having people hate him at first glance.

Which was what Trent felt as he pulled the car onto an area of flattened earth off the side of the road, a few metres from Nahuel Rock. Farouk was leaning against the frame of a jeep, sucking on the end of a joint; the jeep's headlights pooled in the space by the Rock.

Trent popped open the driver-side door and paused to look at the other man, whilst his left hand reached for the gun beside him: a particle-chunker. His brain was still spinning from the collision on the road but he focused on this moment. Farouk thought he was here to do a deal about recruiting girls from the local Ro-Gong Academy; it had been easy to set up. Farouk was a pimp, an abuser of young women and had taken an unhealthy and obsessive interest in Krysta – who was barely nineteen. Farouk had no idea Trent had been fucking her for the last few days.

"As-Salaam-Alaikum," Farouk greeted, his ugly face sneering around the stubby remains of the joint. "Nice wheels. Shame you messed the hood on something." Trent had no interest in talking. He rose up from the Sarotik and brought the particle-chunker out from beside him. Farouk saw it and reacted in a flash, dropped into a full-sprint – heading right for him. Trent pulled the trigger, felt the sub-sonic backwash as the chunker released its charge. Watched Farouk's head vanish in a mist of blood and mincemeat illuminated in the glare of the headlights, saw the body collapse forwards and tumble to the ground like a sack.

Silence. The trees mute in their judgement of his actions.

And then a huge figure was beside him. No time to turn the gun. Only time for a sharp glance, eyes and head snapping round to see what looked like a silhouette with twin suns burning where a face should have been.

"What the -?!"

***

Trent tried to step back but the figure lunged forward with impossible speed, grabbed the arm holding the particle chunker and then got a hand on his groin. It felt like steel pistons closing around his testicles. Trent screamed. The figure hoisted him bodily up from the ground as if he weighed nothing.

"Trent Faber!" the voice was an animalistic shout.

"Ah! JESUS! Do I ... Do I *know* you?!" He hated how high-pitched his voice sounded.

A blunt laugh. "Do you know why Krysta Stine likes you?"

Trent got a whiff of sweat through the pervasive smell of the trees and something else – like the abattoir his step-mother worked at but more...unwholesome. "Krysta? What's this got to do with her?"

"Use your head boy not your cock. It's so she can *use* you. That's all she does. Think about that next time before you pull the trigger."

Next time...?

Trent tried to speak but nothing but a yelp came out as the massive figure hefted him further up as if about to slam him down on the ground like a pro-wrestler.

"Not that you'll remember." The animal voice boomed. The creature that wore the skin of human beings whenchoosing to be amongst them, threw Trent Faber in a violent display of metaphysical power. Not down but back, back through the interlocking vortices of Space and Time.

***

Krysta Stine curled a bare leg around his lower limb beneath the table of the diner. The place was quiet this time of night. Just a few regulars who used it more like a social club with coffee and pancakes. Her hand rested at the top of his thigh and the pressure of her fingertips was making his groin ache to the point where he thought it might explode.

"So you're really going to do it?" she whispered in his ear; the smell of her was like candy floss at the circus carried on the musk of sex.

"Got everything I need," he told her, keeping his eyes fixed on the coffee cup in front of him. What she was wearing was like something from a fantasy sim-stim. He needed to keep his mind on the task ahead. "But don't talk about it here. I'll meet you after. Where are you going to be?"

Krysta was without doubt the most attractive girl he had ever known. And also the strangest. He knew she was dangerous, that her mind harboured secret desires he couldn't possibly understand – never mind fulfil. But he loved her beyond the insane cravings for sex that she constantly invoked.

Her teeth came together around the lobe of his ear, and he could sense her smiling as she bit hard enough to make him flinch.

The regulars looked his way; some saw an older man in love with a much younger girl; others sensed the off-kilter dynamic and bad energy. He didn't react. He'd seen it enough times from people the last few days. His gaze remained anchored to the coffee cup.

"Where are you going to be?" he asked again.

"Come to Smileys. I'll be waiting there."

Trent left the diner and walked to the stolen Sarotik where he'd left it parked in a darkened bay beside a closed book shop.Climbing into the driver-side he popped the panel of the small storage pod and took out the particle-chunker, placed it on the seat beside him then checked the time. Nearly eleven o'clock.

The rendezvous took place at midnight, just as he had planned. It all went like clock- work. Mid-week and this time of night, almost nothing on the roads to cause problems along the way. Maybe it was the fact he'd chosen Wapasha Ridge – familiarity despite the spooky vibe. Even killing a man like Farouk Abdl Musa in cold blood had barely dented his sense of well-being.

But getting to Smiley's he found Krysta Stine wrapped around some guy in road-dirty leathers, prison tattoos and the logos of the Wayra Skulls glowing through the grime. There was a whole bunch of them, crowded around her like she was a priestess.

Queen bee flirting with the drones.

Her eyes caught his across the bare wooden floor, and in the glare of cheap neon bar signs he felt the ice of that gaze.

They were through. She had used him, and now he realised he had somehow always known.

Smiley's wasn't the place to cause trouble. And messing with the Wayra was just a shortcut to getting killed.

He backed away before anyone really noticed him. His hand snaked under the edge of his Lamolux jacket but the particle-chunker wasn't there. Panic rising, he hurried back to the car. But the gun wasn't there either.

His memory replayed shooting Farouk. The headless body tumbling forward into the ground. He'd dropped back into the car and driven away at a controlled speed. Maybe the particle-chunker fell out of the car before he closed the door?

Shit!

He'd have to go back. If the police found the gun they could potentially connect it back to him.

Fate was tugging at his brain. His hands moved over the controls. Started the engine. Feet feeding fuel to the machine.

Like Bolinas, Wapasha Ridge wasn't sign-posted. People had to know it was there to go there.

He was acutely aware of the trees and how close they hemmed in the road.

It felt strange to be back so soon after what he'd done.

He struggled to keep his anxiety in check.

The jeep was still there, headlights blazing against the massive shape of Nahuel Rock. The body was lying where it had fallen. Trent didn't give it more than a glance. He parked up just off the side of the road and started to scan the area he pulled onto before.

Where the hell is the gun?

It was the absolute silence that made him pause after a few moments. The utter lack of any sound.

And then a huge figure was beside him. No time to turn. A sharp glance, eyes and head snapping round to see what looked like a silhouette with twin suns burning where a face should have been.

"Hey!" Trent lashed out with his fists but the man just grabbed Trent with mighty hands, with such violence and strength that Trent felt the world spin around him. He'd been hoisted up into the air.

"I told you to think twice about pulling that trigger boy." Trent squawked and grunted as he tried to get his wordsout; "What the – man, do I fucking *know you*?"

The giant shook him like a broken toy, "I didn't toss you back this time Trent. I broke the loop. Enough time wasted on you. I've got other angles to try."

It took many moments to recover: "How – how do you know my name?"

"Krysta Stine could have been happy with a man like Farouk. Happy enough until Farouk killed her in a black-stim. The whole world would have been different. You know that? No, I don't suppose you can possibly know. Now she'll end up in Paris. And she'll meet Augustus Northcutt – and then everything will change."

"You're fucking crazy man!"

"Inside this skin I wear there's a part of all of you in me. So I care. *I* care, Trent. But even those close to gods must lose their patience in the end."

Trent tried to speak but nothing but a yelp came out as the massive figure hefted him further up as if about to slam him down on the ground like a pro-wrestler.

"Goodbye Trent." The man boomed.

Falling without moving.

A glimpse of immense spheres sliding over each other in the wash of radiation and cosmic currents against a background of infinite emptiness. His eyes wide with disbelief as his mouth howled at the madness of it all.

Darkness.

Hard surface beneath his feet. He moved, unsteady, uncertain of where he was. The ground was broken up. Pot-holed. And then the pungent smell of the forest told him exactly where he was.

Twin Xenon beams punched away the darkness. He saw the road flare into sight ahead of him. Behind him: the savage purr of a custom-made engine being fed the fuel of its life. Too fast for him to move. Just enough time to register this was his end.

BIOGRAPHIES

Chris Halliday is a writer, role-playing game designer and occultist. He lives in Bristol with a very large collection of both books and Daleks, and likes confusing passing aircraft with his big shiny head. He subscribes to the Adams Theory of Aerodynamic Deadlines.

Officially, I first met Dave Rodger back in 2008, six months after accidentally web-stalking him (a story for another time, perhaps). I was lucky enough to join his Yellow Dawn role-playing campaign, through which David enjoyed tormenting his players in all sorts of awful ways. My character entered the campaign escaping from a locked car-trunk. In handcuffs. In a city full of fast-moving zombies. David, of course, thought this was hysterical. He was a notorious practical joker, and he loved to make us squirm.

David and his wide circle of friends became an essential part of my life in Bristol, and in many ways I believe that David was Bristol, in the same way that H.P. Lovecraft declared himself to be Providence. Certainly she seems a wounded place without him. He understood the city in a way few people do, and he loved to share her. Through him I learned her secrets and her curious ways. We'd brainstorm stories together on long walks around the harbourside, drink beer on summer evenings outside the Arnolfini, play board games at the Grain Barge. David and his friends were there for me when life turned on me, and it's no exaggeration to say that between them, they saved my life. He encouraged all of us and celebrated our successes as his own.

David gave the people that mattered to him names. Oj, Sharky Bones McCoy, HIAB-X, Nice Guy Tony, Doctor Nano, Game Breaker Hagen... I knew I'd truly arrived in Bristol when I got mine. I was

Doctor Tic-Toc, then Mr Sardonic, and at the very last, Chris the Lord. That last one was down to a misprint on the program for his funeral that had us snort-laughing through our tears. I like to think he arranged that; one last practical joke from somewhere beyond the rainbow, a reminder not to take life too seriously.

David, this is for you.

Thomas David Parker was born in Bristol, but was quickly exiled to the Forest of Dean so his childhood could be shaped into an Enid Blyton novel. From a young age he discovered a joy of stories and was drawn to the realms of fantasy and the supernatural. His earliest influence was Terry Pratchett, but later joined by Neil Gaiman and M. R. James.

He currently lives in a luxury bachelor pad, where he spends his time writing short stories, editing podcasts, and terrifying his mother that he'll never settle down. He is a member of the Stokes Croft Writers and co-host of Talking Tales, a bi-monthly podcast/ local storytelling event.

I first met David at BristolCon Fringe, where he was reading his short story, Shadow of the Black Sun. The story was good and he was a charismatic figure, so I approached him afterwards and complimented him on his story. David was always pleased to meet new people and asked me lots of questions about my own writing and interests. I had only just started writing, but he soon motivated me to finish my first ever ghost story. His encouragement and belief in me pushed me to write more stories, and get a few published. I owe a lot of my success to David. He always pushed people to fulfil their potential and I'll always be grateful for him as a mentor as well as a friend. He is, and always shall be, deeply missed.

Ian Millsted writes science fiction, horror and well any genre; he's even written a western. His story 'House Blood' received an honourable mention from Ellen Datlow in her 'Best New Horror' series. His novel 'Silence Rides Alone' was published by Sundown Press in 2016 and his critical study 'Black Archives 8: Black Orchid' came out from Obverse Books in 2016.

The last time I saw David was unexpected. I was used to seeing David at readings or pub meets but on that day he was in the post office in the Galleries in Bristol. He was there to post off copies of some of his books to lucky folk who had won a competition on his website. This was one of the few times when I didn't mind the length of time it takes to get to the front of the queue as it gave time to catch up. We mostly talked about the numerous projects that David had bubbling away. I admit to being slightly envious. We parted assuming we would see each other in the pub sometime. I went back to the office. I like to think David went off to enjoy a fine coffee somewhere.

Cheryl Morgan is a writer, editor and critic. Her fiction has appeared in *Holdfast Magazine* and in various anthologies. She has won four Hugo Awards, though none for fiction. Mostly she is happy making better writers than her shine. She owns Wizard's Tower Press and loves bringing good books to eager readers.

I didn't know David well. The closest contact I had with him was when he read at BristolCon Fringe. As the host of the event, it is my job to get to know the readers and make them look good. David and I clearly had a bunch of interests in common. Most importantly we both loved the Cthulhu Mythos and role-playing games. He struck me as someone I would enjoy spending time with. I never got the chance.

Dave Sharrock: *If there's one thing I remember about Dave, it was his unmatched ability to tell a good story. Whether he was describing his brush with Russian mafiosa in a nightclub in Moscow, revealing the latest plot twist in one of his roleplaying games, writing in his blog or producing a book, story telling was in his heart, body and soul. So I can think of no more fitting a tribute than a collection of stories told in Dave's memory and in a style Dave would enjoy.*

Simon Brake is a designer by day, fan of weird fiction by night, and one of several writers/editors at Stygian Fox in the impossible moments in between. You can (and should!) follow him on Twitter at @psibreaker, and you can follow Stygian Fox (@StygianFoxHQ) for all the latest on their work in gaming.

One of the biggest regrets I have is that I never met David face to face. We met across the internet, back at a time before Facebook and Twitter had really kicked off. I was an avid fan of the Call of Cthulhu game (as, indeed, I still am), but in particular had been working on a project to collect and collate information about the mysterious King in Yellow. One of my excursions across the internet brought me to David's virtual doorstep, trying to find out just what this Yellow Dawn was all about, and what the Age of Hastur entailed. And so our online friendship developed. I remember introducing a group of my friends to his zombie-ridden world, but also remember with delight hearing how he transplanted a Call of Cthulhu scenario of my own devising into his world for his own players to experience. And, of course, I loved his stories, and his turns of phrase, and would occasionally ask him for feedback about the stuff I wrote. The last conversation I had with David online was about a scenario I was going to write, specifically for Yellow Dawn. We bounced a few ideas back and forth and thrashed out a few details until we had something that we both were excited about. I never managed to get that scenario finished. When I was invited to contribute to this anthology, I decided that I owed David this one. The Lost Brother is an attempt to mix a young man's reflection on life beyond an earth shattering apocalypse with the mystery of what horror stalks the woods by night. May the stars guide you safely home.

John Houlihan has been a writer, journalist and broadcaster for over twenty five years, working in news, sport, videogames, and latterly roleplaying, board and fantasy games. He has been worked for *The Times, Sunday Times* and *Cricinfo,* was PC editor at *GameSpot* and is a former editor-in-chief of *Computer and Video Games.com.* He currently works as narrative designer of Achtung! Cthulhu for Modiphius and is editor-in-chief of *Dragon+* the official Dungeons & Dragons magazine for Wizards of the Coast. He's published *The Trellborg Monstrosities, The Crystal Void, Tomb of the Aeons* and *Before the Flood*in his Seraph Chronicles series, as well as a novel, *Tom or the Peepers' and Voyeurs' Handbook,* and *The Cricket Dictionary,* a humorous guide to the phrases and sayings of the greatest of all games. He's also editor of *Dark Tales from the Secret War,* a collection of World War 2 Cthulhu themed stories. More @john259 or at www.john-houlihan.net.

I first met David at Future's Bath office, when some publisher's latest random project connected us. We quickly discovered our shared love of Lovecraft, sci-fi and fantasy writing, and resolved to form the League of Cthulhu, a mutual support group to help each other share the writerly burden. What I remember most about David, is his kindness and generosity towards an emerging fellow scribbler. He was always supremely supportive and encouraging, generous

*to a fault and a great man to bounce the wildest of ideas off. We
rarely met in person, but talked all the time online. They say every
man's death diminishes us, but some diminish us more than others.
I miss him a great deal naturally, but we're all that much poorer for
the absence of his soaring, visionary mind.*

Samantha J. Rule grew up pursuing various arts, martial,
writing, painting, and sewing. In her spare time, she likes to brew
beer and ponder the meaning of life, the universe, and everything.
After a nomadic upbringing in a military family, she has called
the desert of Northern Arizona home for over a decade where she
currently resides and writes with her husband and soul mate,
Eli Johnston.

Eli Johnston was introduced to fiction writing by his mother,
a published author in her own right, at the age of two. He grew up,
travelled the world, completed his professional terminal degree, and
then married the love of his life. Eli spends his leisure time helping
her tend to their southwest garden, which is often overgrown with
habanero's and other chili peppers of note.

*I met David through the web in 2009. We met through words.
He would say, "Paint me a picture with words when you write me
back." Which then turned into "Send words when inspired." We
continued to paint pictures with words back and forth in letters, our
daily lives grown majestic and atmospheric in their retellings. He
was ceaselessly encouraging, inspiring, and a source of positive
energy. David was a curator of moments, of good people, and of
words. I hope you enjoy what we've "painted" for you, David.. Love
& Light, Sir.*

Dave Bradley was born in west London in the grimdark murk
of the 1970s, studied medieval literature before moving to Bath in
1997 to become a magazine journalist. He paid his dues writing
for, and then editing, home computing and video gaming titles. In
2005 he took the helm of SFX, the UK's top sci-fi magazine. It was
while working at Future Publishing, running SFX and sister titles
Comic Heroes and Crime Scene, that Bradley crossed paths with
David Rodger. Having always written for personal pleasure, in the
last few years Bradley began sharing his short stories with a local
writing/drinking group. He is grateful for their encouragement,
and that of David Rodger himself whose creativity was infectious.

Bradley now lives in Wiltshire and works as an editorial consultant, currently helping Steel Media run websites and international events for mobile game developers.

The first time I met David Rodger it was in All Bar One in Bath. David had joined the team that oversaw SFX's website; mutual friends at Future Publishing realised that we had a lot in common, and encouraged us to meet. David suggested a lunchtime coffee, and that would turn into the first of many such meetings. The Raven and the Boston Tea Party became the regular haunts for us. "Lunch with The Rodge" just appeared in my office calendar from time to time. Such was his energy and drive that I got way more out of the meetings than he did. Soon I would anticipate our lunches as times when he'd inspire me to write, or travel, or play games, or just relax better. I can still hear his voice in my head offering me fiction advice... or insisting I try the kedgeree. (I suspect he was the unofficial guardian of the Boston Tea Party's menu, even galvanising a few of us into campaigning when kedgeree was removed from their list.) David was generous with his time and experience. Once, when I told him I didn't know how to get started with a story, he gave me all his notes from a novel he'd been working on so I could follow his authorial process. I'm very proud to appear in the acknowledgements of his novel The Social Club. But a confession: I've not read it yet. Because that means it's still there on a shelf, like a brand new David J Rodger book I can look forward to.

Pete Sutton has a not so secret lair in the wilds of Fishponds, Bristol and dreams up stories, many of which are about magpies. He's had stuff published, online and in book form, including a short story collection called A Tiding of Magpies (Shortlisted for the British Fantasy Award 2017) and the novel Sick City Syndrome. He wrote all about Fishponds for the Naked Guide to Bristol and has made more money from non-fiction than he has from fiction and wonders if that means the gods of publishing are trying to tell him something. Pete is a member of the North Bristol Writers.

You can find him all over social media or worrying about events he's organised at the Bristol Festival of Literature, Bristol HorrorCon and BristolCon. On Twitter he's @suttope and he's published by Kensington Gore http://www.kensingtongorepublishing.com/pete-sutton/4591911186

DAVID J RODGER:
SOME MEMORIES:
NOV 5TH 2016
BROOKLYN
FLOYD HAYES

My recollection of meeting David for the first time is blurry. I can't quite pin it down. We were both from Newcastle and had some mutual acquaintances. Newcastle, being Newcastle, we must have crossed paths numerous times. At 1980s teenage house parties, at the various haunts around the city: The Monument, St. George's, Hippy Green, Pet's Cemetery, The Riverside...

In High School, he lived next to a girl I had a crush on for a while. The kind of crush, where you just walk past their house in the hope they will happen to look out - and in that instant, fall deeply in love with you. I didn't realize I was also walking past a person who would become much more important to me than a fleeting fancy.

The first time we officially met must have been in Dalston, North London, somewhere around 1998. I was living with Grassy, who he also knew well. There is a photo of me, lying on the floor, blissed out and grinning sloppily up at the camera. I was shocked to see this picture on his blog many years after the incident. I hadn't realized he'd taken it until then.

My relationship with him was certainly off-beat at times (in the best way), and often involved cameras and odd snatches of suddenly in focus memories.

One of these memories occurs as I write this. The place: the original World Headquarters club, the time: somewhere between 1990-something and the early Naughties.

The date is nebulous but the memory is sharp. I was dancing with him in the centre of the tiny, girl-packed dance floor. And I mean REALLY dancing, going nuts and throwing ridiculous dance shapes about the place and totally getting into it, facing each other, grinning intently at one another, A mutual feeling of a deep, fast-friendship forming and one of those powerful moments of being aware that, 'this is it, this is our time!' It was and it was.

He had that ability, to sweep you up and into a positive space, a place of possibilities.

He had prescient abilities too. Just one example would be the DV Frames that appear in a few of his stories, they predated Microsoft's HoloLens by many, many years. His work is full of these predictive glimpses of the future. His art was to mix them with ancient lore, action, suspense, horror and three dimensional (sometimes trans-dimensional) characters, all set within a far-reaching vision of the fate of humanity.

He also foresaw the growing popularity of zombies. His version of them is still my favourite. When I get enough internal strength, I'm looking forward to re-reading 'Living in Flames.' His vision of the genre was (and is) totally unique, much like the man himself. I often wondered (but never asked) if this massive interest around one of his core writing themes bothered him. It must have been frustrating to see this element of his work become so huge in pop culture. His take on the undead was so much richer, more interesting, way weirder and just down-right cooler than others.

In 2004, I moved to NYC. David and I became closer friends from this point, despite the physical distance between us. Being huge Sci-Fi fans, I think we both got a kick out of using technology to grow our friendship. We'd email often.

I became a big fan of his blog which had a 'hidden window' buried in the flames of a background image. It would take his inner circle into the photos and the more personal musings he posted. I loved this idea. One of his many quirky imaginative sparks that have set my mind alight over the time I had the pleasure of getting to know him. He still inspires me and I'm still getting to know him now. That thought has just given me a sense of unexpected happiness, although these days he won't answer my damn emails. I like to think he's probably busy but will get back to me one day...

Recently, I searched for his name in my emails, to read through old correspondence and see if there was, I don't know, anything there, a clue, something I'd missed or... I don't know....

So many musings on David just end in questions that I can't properly define or find answers to. I wish the bastard was here so I could ask him!

Along with emailing, we'd also randomly call one another and we had a special text ritual too.

I'm jumping about. I'm terrible with dates and the order of things. Somehow, that seems appropriate, the confusion, the tangled feelings. So many good feelings too.

In the States, I believe the first book I bought of his was 'God Seed.' I remember buying it out of solidarity, perhaps dreading it would be bad and I'd have to lie to him. I needn't have worried.

The way I read his work repeated across all his books. I'd devour them in two massive sessions, finding it hard to just walk away from it.

A later book, 'Edge really blew me away. I couldn't believe I knew anyone personally who wrote work of this calibre. Frankly, it was a bit of a turn-on but also intimidating. I knew we'd discuss his work, but me being me, I'd forget tons of detail the moment I finished reading. It was nothing personal, just the way I am. "What was the main dude's name again?" I always felt like I was doing DJR a disservice.

I do recall finishing Edge and literally jumping up and down on my roof one summer in Williamsburg, Brooklyn. I was so convinced and excited about his talent. I vividly remember, later that night, standing up in the back garden of Iona, (an Irish bar) and loudly asking the large group of buzzed strangers if anyone there was a book publisher or agent. I had to laugh when three people piped up in the affirmative. 'So New York.'

I struck up conversations and friendships with two of them. I bought more books and pushed them into their hands. I wanted so badly for David to be 'discovered.' Admittedly, It was my ego too, imagine if I was the guy to break him here, the movies, the gaming, the toys! It'd be awesome!

He came to the States and I recall two particular occasions, I'm struggling to remember the dates (what a surprise). I believe I met him at the Port Authority Station. A grim place much brightened by David striding up and gripping my hand and the customary greeting, "Hey brother!"

He'd brought along a friend who (unbeknownst to me) he was trying to set me up with. A night of drinking commenced. We sat in the Ear Inn, West of SoHo. The perfect venue for him, a place full of old stories, myths, demons and decent ales. We sat under the clock on the wall and DJR took another photo of me. This later became my professional profile pic for years over at LinkedIn and it appeared in tons of keynote biography documents.

It was a rare night. We spoke of all the mutual things we loved, mostly imaginative flights of fancy and the planning of weird schemes. One of my favourite collaborative ideas was being hatched then. I'd planned to open a real 'socially responsible' marketing agency called The Social Club (TSC).

It would be ten percent fictional, which he'd write. We'd never admit to the fiction, it was part of the game we wanted to play. Some of the work on our (real) website would be made up, shadowy government agency work, hints at something strange and otherworldly. These exploits would carry on in the books and blogs he wrote (I think there are a few posts alluding to this). In the meantime, I'd reflect his fiction into client work and the real world. It was ridiculous and a lot of fun. I think we were attempting to lay down the foundations of a benign business cult. This came to fruition in his novel, 'The Social Club.' It was sort of in jest and sort of not... that was one of the many things I loved about David, you could blend the lines between fact and fiction, visit different planets of thought and merge them together. That sense of possibility and boundlessness. Few people give me that feeling and man, I miss it.

At some point around this time his book 'Edge' was passed onto William Gibson via me hassling a friend who was in line to get his autograph at Barnes & Noble in Union Square, Manhattan (yeah, that's the kind of PR pro I was). Gibson, upon being handed the book, simply said, "Thanks." I toyed with the idea of printing some posters for Edge with the quote 'Thanks' by Gibson on it, as a sort of joke/weak PR stunt.

By this time David was referring to me as his New York agent. It was kind of an in-joke but I really did want to get him known, and I ran around getting meetings and evangelizing his work to my meagre clutch of literary contacts. In my heart-of-hearts I know I really didn't try hard enough and it's something I regret. I had excuses, a young daughter, the challenge of trying to survive in NYC, just getting rent paid while staying sane. I once apologized for my poor results and his response made me feel good, he told me he was glad to have a contact out here and there was no pressure. He was happy to just say he had an agent in New York.

He deserved better.

Come to think of it, he didn't have a bad word to say about people - behaviour yes - but never people.

Again, my timelines are all getting crossed but one vivid memory emerged. We met in Newcastle once again. It's odd how often we both seemed to meet there, without planning, me being in NYC, he in Bristol, slowly flowing to the bridge next to the Old Mill in Jesmond Dene.

This one particular time, we met in the Jesmond Dene House, a little bit of a fancy venue, but we liked the pose. Both now being men of the world and (seemingly) doing well in our own corners of it. The environs suited a particularly playful, successful version of ourselves we were cultivating at the time. Members of TSC, with my feet dipping into corporate America and with him unspooling a new and terrifying future vision through his books. It was weird and not to mention fun as we sat and constructed all these crazy narratives, building a peculiar new reality for ourselves. Few people ever made me feel like that apart from David, of being in a living story, a more thrilling version of my actual day-to-day life.

We walked through the Dene and he showed me the place where a gruesome scene in one of his books occurred near the old chapel (Dog Eat Dog?) It was a fantastically unnerving moment, stood in the spot and recalling the scene in the story. The sudden coalescence of fantasy, reality, imagination and future possibilities. It was so 'us.'

We walked down to the Mill and here he told me the origin of the name Jesmond Dene / Jesus Mound and The Apparition of Mary. I loved David when these strange tales would emerge, these peculiar, Lovecraftian glimpses into the oddness pressing around us all. It was never grim or depressing, David delighted in it and this in term brought light into the darker corners of the world.

Speaking of which, there was a time (it may have been on the same day, or not) when I really did blow his mind for once (it was almost always the other way round).

I asked if he wanted to walk over to 'Devil's Canyon.'

"Where?" he asked, genuinely puzzled.

"The Old Quarry, A.K.A. The Devil's Canyon, you must know it!"

He looked blank. Weird. It's a well-known spot at the end of the Dene. A place of illicit smoking, occasional skanky rave parties, gothic occultism, rock climbing and general ne'er-do-well skulking. It's genuinely creepy and unsettling, never getting full sunlight. Exactly the kind of place David would have gotten a kick out of.

So, we walked there; through the dark green light and the musty smell of the Ouesburn.

We walked into the little canyon. David's face and behaviour were something to behold. It was like watching someone experiencing a hard wave of acid hitting their system, the kind you feel too, just standing near them, like a psychic ripple. It can't be faked.

He'd never known this whole part of the Dene had existed despite living near it his entire life. It was a weird and magical moment. Like showing someone Narnia in their own wardrobe.

Other Dene moments, and there seemed to be many, but never enough as it turned out...

I switched him on to a slightly shameful behaviour of mine called 'Ghosting.' I'd basically lie to everyone I know about times and dates of leaving and arriving places. I'd do it to eke out a secret day to myself. A ghost day. He was the only person I'd be straight with about this or want to spend ghost days with. David was like that, I could be totally honest with him. Rather, he brought it out of me. A talent of great writers I think.

We'd arrange to meet at the Mill Bridge as per. Another photo of me by him, perhaps the last one he took of me and it's one of my faves. I look tired but also happy to be with the person on the other side of the lens.

We'd often walk up to the upper parts near Paddy Freeman's fields. There, he'd scramble down a bit of the hill and give a meaningful and deeply felt hug to a particular tree. I never asked why and we never spoke about it. It was endearing and singularly David.

From then on, when one of us was in Newcastle, we'd go to the Mill and text, 'Greetings from the Dene.' I'd love to get a random ping from David with this message as I hurried up Madison Avenue or had to deal with some New York headache or other... I wish for those messages now.

Another memory: It must have been just after 2010. I'd watched my Gran die and was in a mess. I met with David in Whitley Bay. There was a hip flask involved. I'm pretty sure he stripped naked and dived into the brutally cold North Sea in the winter. It was mad and funny, a beautifully off-beat distraction at a much needed time.

His second visit to me in New York. Date again unknown, was unforgettable.

There was a kind of 'nexus point' I wanted to get to with him. I read many of his books on my own at my house in the foothills of the Catskill mountains, upstate New York. A place that inspired Lovecraft, who was of course a big influence on DJR's work. I loved the idea of having him up at the house, his books, the brooding mountains, the shadow of Lovecraft.

I wanted to take him to the Country Inn, about 50-mins down a tree shrouded lane from my house. I didn't drive at the time, so despite the hammering rain, we walked. We didn't care, it felt like an adventure. We arrived at the Inn soaked to the skin and were greeted by a huge, almost violent wood fire. It was early and we were the only people there. We stood, backs to the fire, steam rising from us like one of those manhole covers in Manhattan. We talked and drank. A very good moment in time.

If David's passing has taught me anything, it's to appreciate these small moments of happiness with people.

On the walk back David asked if I minded him wearing headphones. No of course not. It was pitch dark and the rain was still incessant. Warmed by the fire and the ales, we marched stoically though the slamming sheets of water.

I learned that night that David would 'anchor' key moments in music, he'd pick particular tracks to listen to and fix the moment and the mood in his mind, to be recalled later by playing back that music track. A brilliant trick, such a considered way to use music and memory. I often refer to it.

A side note, I was also vaguely jealous of his old MP3 player. It was a stand-alone unit requiring one AA battery. Comparatively ancient tech and out of sorts for a Sci-Fi writer, but somehow exactly right.

The following day is something I will never forget. I had to order a cab to get us to Kingston bus station, a 45-minute drive. I'd just started using some tiny operation as the main cab service is appalling and always late. On this particular occasion, the usual guy wasn't driving. No worries, he said he knew the esoteric route to the station.

We jump in the back. It was puzzling how the driver couldn't seem to back out of te driveway. Admittedly, the angle is peculiar and many people have to go at it a couple of times but this seemed excessive.

Once straightened up, we got on our way. Like all local drivers, he went too fast for comfort around the up and down, narrow and curvy country roads. Every corner blind. Speeding along County Route 2, both David and I noticed a large SUV backing out of a driveway suddenly 15ft in front of us. Weird how terrifying moments seem to play out in slow motion. He's going to see the car right? 9ft. Right?! 2ft. Right?!!

I will never know how we missed it. It was so close, not a foot close, we are talking less than half an inch. We seemed to pass through it. It was a deeply disturbing incident, leaving us pale and shaking, adrenalin stabbing hard. Afterwards, we half joked that it had been impossible to miss the car, and we had both died or had been jolted 'out of the simulation.' (another fave topic of ours over the years).

Back in the car. Now on the highway. Our breathing returning to normal from panic panting, adrenalin climbing down from Def Con 1. Then David nudged me, we looked at the driver in the rear view, he was asleep! Fecking asleep! The car was drifting into the centre line, no barriers, we we're headed straight into the speeding on-coming traffic. There's lot of shouting and demanding to be pulled over and let out. The driver jolted awake but refused to stop.

Real life horror.

We called the cab controller guy, threatening to get the cops if he didn't get this guy off the road immediately.

I still sweat when I think about this journey but it was a hell of a bonding moment between David and I.

We often referred to that experience in morbid fascination and relief.

More recently, 2014, I visited David and Jo in Bristol. Here is the post from my (poorly written) diary from the time. I won't edit out of vanity. Note, I reread bits of my diary and sometimes make comments and edits, I'll leave them in too. I should say that David's blogging style inspired a lot of how I chronicle stuff.

Diary Entry Starts

Saturday November 25th, 2013: Train

"Looking forward to seeing David. He is one of those people I 'channel' when I need strength. He's a good man. A singular kind of fella, doesn't suffer fools and knows what he wants, needs and how to get it. The opposite of me. :)"

Sunday November 24th, 2013: Bristol DJR

"Arrived in Bristol after a pleasant, no hassle journey. Took a very short cab ride to the Shakespeare tavern to listen to David's reading from The Social Club book. Nice old boozer with a good crowd of folks."

{edit Nov 5th 2016. I was nervous that day. TSC was an elaborate plan we both had been developing for a while. I wanted to play the part of a character here, one of the TSC inner circle, with shades of Scientology. Sounds odd now but we were aiming for a mixed media/alt reality game and this was the first time to sort of try it out. I drank about 4 beers very quickly and immediately regretted it. I can fake professionalism and play games well, but not when I'm blurry. It was the first time I'd met a lot of his friends. He read well and looked very sharp in his suit, I felt extremely proud of him that day. There was a Q&A after DJR's fine reading and I asked something banal. I felt angry at myself for not being a better 'wing man' or playing my assigned part well. At the same time, I was made to feel really welcome by all his amazing friends but that feeling of letting him down has somehow stuck with me from that afternoon. [end edit]

"A few more ales and a trip to a cocktail bar for one before heading to the chippy for one of the biggest pieces of cod I've managed to eat. We settled down in front of the fire and chatted, played a fantastic game called the Journey on the PS3.

Just woke up now in the Attic room, it's late and it's cold. Looking forward to a coffee and a walk around the harbor."

6:00pm

"In David's living room, fire just starting, radio playing through TV. We took a decent walk around the harbour in Bristol, via a legal graffiti mural area.

Historic, nice day, stopped for a greasy spoon brunch. We settled in a barge bar, on a leather sofa, DJR dozing and writing, drinking a hot chocolate. He gave me an Alan Moore book to read. Two light ales and a horror book done, we walked into town, jumped into a taxi before grabbing a vindaloo curry ready to settle and watch one of his movies, likely a classic horror. All good."

[edit Oct 6th, 2016, 2:15am : the film was The Ninth Gate. The first and last movie I watched with DJR. I watched it again fairly recently in memory of him and had forgot how the film started, not good. I don't have the words right now. I think of him often. I suspect this was the last time I saw him but we always chatted and emailed regularly, right up until the week before. He told me he wasn't in a good place. I asked him to come over to the house upstate, I wish I could remember the call better."[end edit]

{edit Nov 5th, 2016 That moment in the barge was one of the times I will always remember the most fondly. It was one of those 'peak happines' moments. It was busy but we had the best seats. David sat next to me with his giant leather notebook (I called it his Necronomicon). He dozed a little and I poured through the gruesome horror graphic novel. I was never one to really love horror but he certainly got me into it more, and for that I thank him. I'd never considered reading HPL before meeting him either, another piece of the never ending inspirations and tips for good stuff. It was so warm there and the beer was good, the light was perfect, I felt so relaxed and at peace with David. One of those rare people who I can just sit with, not talking, just being happy and content.

At the time of the funeral, I arrived at the station and went to the Shakespeare wondering what I would feel, would there be a sense of David, would I cry my eyes out, have some kind of revelation? I went in, it was a bit quiet, the staff were vaguely rude like last time. I had a beer and wandered about. Looked at the spot where DJR had read from TSC. I felt numb. Not even. Just nothing. [end edit]

Diary Entry Ends

In a slightly odd or even macabre twist - at the time of David's funeral, two years later, I'd booked a Bristol hotel at random from the States. True to the 'tradition' I had with David, I booked earlier than needed and 'Ghosted' a day in Bristol.

I got to the hotel and checked in. Slung my bag down and wondered what to do with myself.

I looked out the window and straight onto the barge and could see the seats where I'd last been with David. It was so typical of our relationship. Weird encounters and odd blurry almost scripted happenings. I smiled. I imaged David giving a tight smile too, wherever he was.

I've probably talked as much about myself as about David here. This is typical me, I can only apologise but I hope some of who he was and what he meant to me has shone through my dull writing.

I also shared some of the 'darker' moments but that's how it was. David always made any situation just more interesting, thought provoking and that's something I hang onto and appreciate about knowing him.

He was a big influence. I still channel him regularly. I go to the Ear on an occasion and think of him. Oh, and I did end up having a short but pleasingly passionate fling with the girl he tried to link me up with , so thanks for that David, always appreciated mate.

I can't bring myself to re-read any of his books yet. I'm saving it. I will do it though, And next time I'm in the Dene I will send my greetings to him from there. Not just greetings, but love and memories. I will remember his stories and perhaps hug a tree.

Essences of him will always be with me. He will be carried into the future via the memory of those who loved him and through the amazing work he left behind.

As time unfolds, his physicality moves into the past and yet he remains, existing in my heart somewhere between reality and fiction, just as he always has.

Rest in peace David, I miss you terribly. Thank you for your continued inspiration.

Floyd. November 9th, 2016, Clinton Hill, Brooklyn, NY.

Lightning Source UK Ltd.
Milton Keynes UK
UKOW04f0830281217

314977UK00001B/43/P

9 780995 464162